"Owning Jolene"

Shelby Hearon

Alfred A. Knopf   New York   1989

THIS IS A BORZOI BOOK
PUBLISHED BY ALFRED A. KNOPF, INC.

Library of Congress Cataloging-in-Publication Data
Hearon, Shelby.
Owning Jolene.
I. Title.
PS3558.E25609   1989   813'.54   88-45261
ISBN 0-394-57175-4

Portions of this novel appeared in earlier versions in
Cosmopolitan and Mississippi Review.

Manufactured in the United States of America
First Edition

FOR BILL,
MY HOME

I wish to thank the
Ingram Merrill Foundation
for its support.

Owning Jolene

1

I'M LEARNING to pose.

At first it made me nervous, standing here with the sheet knotted below my navel, the rest of me with nothing on, holding the hand between my breasts.

I'd forget and slip back into myself—wonder if I was ever going to see L.W. again, or wish it was time to eat—and then Henry would tell me to think about the hand, concentrate on the hand, get rid of everything on my mind but the hand.

Now it's mostly automatic with me, the way it is with Henry when we do it. I don't mean that in a bad way—I never had anybody make love the way he does, and I like it a lot. It's hard to explain, but it's the way people who live with dogs or cats deal with them without ever having to think about it.

You've seen a cat lover sit down, and maybe she's talking to whoever is there about something absolutely major, but because of knowing about cats, her fingers will sort of move by themselves when one walks into the room. She'll scratch against the couch a bit, scratch, scratch, until the cat moseys over to see what's going on. Then she'll move the scratching up to the cushion beside her, hold her fingers out for a sniff, and the first thing you know the cat will be up there, in her lap, and she'll be rubbing it behind the ears and down the back, deciding where to stop her hand if it's in heat and you shouldn't go too far toward the tail, and then she'll concentrate on the best places behind the ears and maybe under the neck if the cat likes that, and pretty soon the cat is digging into her thigh like a kitten kneading its mother, and the purring sounds like an air conditioner on high, and all the while the person is continuing to talk to her friend about this matter of life and death.

What I'm saying is that it isn't *routine*; it's *automatic*.

It doesn't bother me that Henry paints in his head the whole time his body is doing it any more than it bothers me that he has sex while he's painting. And in a way he does. I mean, I see sometimes that he has a hard-on standing there in his drawstring pants and no shirt, and his bony face with the deep eyes has that look that would scare you to death in a man if he touched you looking like that, worrying he wouldn't know when to stop, but I see him working on the canvas, miles away, and I know it means he's on automatic.

When we make love, he makes me come until he sees I'm not going to come any more, when it's reached the way for me that your body feels when you're outside taking a sunbath all warm to your toes with oil, and then your skin feels scratchy and the sun is too hot and you're ready to cool off, or you've been dancing until your feet feel like they can fly and nothing is as wonderful in all the world as dancing, and then you want to sit down and mop up and lean back and gasp for breath a lot. Then Henry comes—which lately is mostly sitting up (he has some ways he likes to do it sitting up)—and when we're through, he wraps me in a sheet and goes to the easel.

Then, if it takes me more than five minutes to sort of snap out of it, wake up and stretch and get ready to pose, I hear him making these noises, setting a glass down or scuffing his feet a lot, and I jump up and hurry in here.

Sometimes I look around the studio to get in the mood. Henry works in a very ordinary house, on a street of ordinary houses (Mom would admire his choice), in a quiet part of the city, but then he's added on a two-story room with an all-window wall on the back so there's a lot of light that has an almost good glare about it, yet at the same time a feeling of privacy, because no one can look in, because the yard has a high screen of bamboo around it. I think about how safe it feels and that I wouldn't mind living here sometime.

But mostly I think about the hand. Its fingers are slightly
spread, the way a little girl would spread them if she were
keeping someone away. It's a hand you could hold up if you
wanted to say, "Stop right there," or "Wait a minute."

Henry says I'm great. That he's never had anybody who
could pose for hours; who didn't fidget. But it's hard for me
to imagine that anyone wouldn't like to stand here with her
mind on just one thing, not having to pay attention to anyone
and with nobody paying attention to her, all morning long.

2

"WE'RE GOING to Purloin Letter it,"
Mom told me the first time we ran away.

She had packed our stuff, our bags and boxes, what we
could take with us, and was putting the finishing touches on
us in the airport bathroom. She'd got this idea that my uncle
Brogan was going to have a description out for us, that he
was tired of her and Dad stealing me back and forth and
meant to keep me at his house.

"This suit's too little," I said.

"You're a four-year-old boy. It fits fine. That's a genuine
Florence Eiseman. I hit on a real bargain. Seventy-five cents."

"I'm a seven-year-old girl."

"Don't be difficult, Jolene. When you're in this Dutch boy
blond wig and that blue suit, you're a four-year-old boy. Now
this is what you'll do. Are you listening to me?"

"I think so."

"A certain man may be waiting out there. I'm referring to
a man named Brogan Temple."

"Uncle—"

"Not uncle. Nobody to you. Nobody you know. He might be the uncle of a certain girl named Jolene Temple, but he is nothing, nobody, a total absolute stranger to four-year-old Sonny. Got that?"

I nodded. "I'm supposed to pretend I don't see him." I looked up, expecting her big toothy grin, the one I got, and her pupils got, when we gave the right answer.

"Wrong." She tugged a wig down on my head, stashing my dark hair under it. "Wrong, wrong, wrong. You are not going to pretend you don't see him, because you aren't going to see him, because you don't know him. You, Sonny, *do not know him.*"

"I don't know Uncle Brogan."

"Christ." She left me with the bags while she went to pee. When she came back, I thought some stranger was trying to pry Mom's purse from between my feet. She had on some jacket thing, I guess also from the thrift shop, and this sort of clinging dress and heels. Now my mom did not even own a pair of heels, and seeing her in them was something like seeing your very first transvestite, something like your very first realization that the woman you're watching has an Adam's apple. Here was my mom in a ton of makeup and these spike-heeled fake skin shoes. She didn't have a wig on, but instead of her hair being held back as usual with the kind of dime store rubber band that's made to look like something else, metallic and shiny, it was down by her face thick and straight. "Rich hair," she said, pleased with the effect. "Brogan could take me to bed and not know it was his sister."

"Where are we going?"

"One thing at a time. We're getting out of here. Then we'll see. I have my eye on a certain suburb. The world is full of neighborhoods just lying there waiting for the plucking."

"What if it's Aunt Glenna Rose out there?"

"Who?" She bent down and stared at me.

"What if it's somebody I don't know, the wife of that man I don't know. *You know,* Mom." I was tired of the game.

"No sweat. She'll be looking anyway for a little crying girl dressed in the pink ruffles she gave you Christmas. But she won't be out there. Glenna Rose is going to be too embarrassed to show up in an airport in her fur coat and grab a kid. That's not her style."

I knew she was right, but I thought I wouldn't mind just then feeling my aunt's arms, furry as a great wild animal, holding me tight as a bear in the Big Thicket, not letting me go, forgetting that she was holding on, talking to Brogan about something else, while he stewed around about how my mom was going to come back and take me, or even my dad. The two of them, Brogan and Glenna Rose, going at it in their big house, with me wrapped in Blackglama and all the air conditioners going full blast, because how else are you going to wear a fur coat in San Antonio, Texas?

"Okay," Mom said, bending down to give me a face full of mothballs. "Okay. Now this is it. We're going to stride right out there through that gate. The only way not to be spotted is to be noticeable. Got it?"

"I think so."

Mom's number one rule was: the best way to hide is to be conspicuous.

When we weren't on the run, she was a piano teacher. A young mother, she would say by way of making her point, moving into a neighborhood of young mothers, comes under instant scrutiny. "What does your husband do, Mrs. Temple? He left eight years ago? Then who is the father of seven-year-old Jolene? You got the dates mixed up? I see." It was not possible, she said, to escape curiosity, comparisons—in short, trouble—if you were the same as everyone else.

But go in *generic,* and immediately your work was done

for you. No one asked piano teachers over for morning coffee; you weren't expected to know which pony park was the pre-school birthday party favorite. Hearing the words "piano teacher," the young mothers instantly attributed to you all the biases and memories of their girlhoods (boyhoods, too, she would add; don't forget all those boys in short pants, aimed for the concert stage, who now sell life insurance), and—in the blink of an eye—you simply disappeared.

"Now, Sonny, here's what you do. When I'm handing the boarding passes to the stewardess, here's what you do. Are you with me?"

I nodded, not as sure it was going to work out as she was.

"The thing to remember is that whoever it is, they'll be looking for a girl. They don't care about me, Midge; they wouldn't a one of them care if they never saw me again. But you, that's the ticket. You're the one. You're their *cause celebrity*," she said, mimicking Aunt Glenna's bad French. "And there's only one way to get past them if they're watching the gate. And they will be, because they know—with my car sitting in the drive with two flats and a dead battery—that we've got exactly two options: we can catch a bus or we can take to the air. My guess is that their guess is a plastic card is easier to use for wings than for heading up IH35.

"Now, here's what you do. They're looking for a little girl, okay? This is crucial. When I hand over our boarding passes—are you getting this, Jolene? When I hand over our boarding passes, you, Sonny, are going to grab your wienie. They're looking for a girl. It's a subliminal trick, see? You grab your wienie and so you're immediately not who they're looking for. Okay? So at that minute—look at me. Pay attention. At that minute you grab your wienie and holler, 'I need to tinkle.'"

3

W H E N I F I R S T got together with Henry,
I thought we would get to be in love. I thought painters were
the kind who would be in love with their models; that I was
the kind who would be in love with a man that I screwed
almost every day.

But it never came to that.

At the start, I had the idea I would be his girlfriend, the
night I met him at the gallery opening and picked him over
the other painters.

So at first I was always nagging him to take me to meet
his folks. I don't know why—I wasn't about to take him to
Brogan and Glenna's, where I lived, on account of his being
their age. And also because Brogan would have taken one
look at Henry and seen that what was going on with us was
not okay by his standards.

But I figured it would be different with Henry's family. He
had been divorced for a long time, from two wives. Surely his
mother and his daughter, who was just a kid (or I thought
that at the time), wouldn't be any problem. I mean, he must
have brought women around to meet them before, in all those
years.

"Just once." I begged him a lot, in the beginning.

"Home and work mix like oil and water," he said. This
was when we were first getting into the sitting-up phase. He
had my head still in his lap, and he hadn't wrapped me in the
sheet yet, and I was feeling sexy all over.

"I want to meet them."

"Forget it."

"Then I'm not going to pose any more."

"Fine with me. I'll check who's hanging out at openings wearing lizard shoes." But I knew he didn't mean it.

Finally, I nagged him until he said, "Okay, there's an exhibit of Southwest stuff this weekend. We can check it out, then have lunch at Mother's. Will that satisfy you?"

He told me to think up a story for my aunt and uncle about why I was going to be gone on Saturday, and to wear my silk suit.

. . .

First we stopped by the Sun Dog art gallery to see a show of what was called Southwest Artifacts. Collected items that Henry said were now considered real antiques, but that to me looked like old cowboy and Indian props. Frontier things that practically created their own stage sets just hanging on the walls or sitting on the floor.

There were gourds and cow skulls—lots of these—and cactus clocks and beaded pouches and cowhide chairs. Then there were some pieces of wooden furniture, sort of standing clothes closets, some of which were priced as high as ten thousand dollars. I couldn't believe it.

I liked best of all an antler-framed mirror; I mean it must have had forty deer antlers all locked together in a circle like a Christmas wreath around this old tin-looking mirror. Henry said if I liked it so much he'd buy it. I thought he was kidding, but in a minute the gallery owner handed it to him, wrapped in orange paper and tied with a string.

Henry also bought a turquoise necklace, which I guessed was for me, too, but I didn't ask, in case it wasn't. Besides, by that time I had the idea that everything was a hundred times more than seemed possible, so I felt bad about hinting for the mirror.

Mostly we stood around and talked to the man who had

brought the show. You couldn't call him an artist, so I guess he was more like a dealer. He talked to Henry about how he had Indian pieces that were going to be worth a fortune one of these days. That he was thinking of making a separate exhibit out of his collection of leather chaps. That he'd already sorted out the boots and the jewelry. That the turquoise necklace and a couple of sets of seed beads were part of this lot, but the rest had gone on to Paris for another show.

Henry wasn't really listening to him. He was looking, studying everything, in the fast way he has. Sometimes asking me to move around and stand by an old fiddle or the cow skulls, or to pretend to wear a pair of spurs, and then moving me somewhere else, all the time the man was talking to him. Maybe the man thought Henry, because of his way of noticing everything, was going to buy a lot. Or maybe he just wanted to have somebody to talk to; there were only two other people in the Sun Dog's orange interior, and they were looking for earrings.

Afterwards, we walked along the river and then up to the streets in the heart of downtown. We passed the HemisFair grounds, and then a tiny restaurant with a Mexican name where about fifty Anglos in business suits, couples, were standing in a long line halfway around the block waiting to get in. Henry said they were all going to eat Saturday's soup, but I didn't know if he was kidding me.

Finally, we turned into this beautiful street of really huge houses. Henry explained this was where the original Germans had settled, the ones with music and education, and that a lot of the same families who had come over back then still lived here. But that his mother wasn't one of these. That he'd bought the house for her a few years ago, after his first big show. But for me not to mention that I knew that she hadn't lived there all her life.

He also said we'd tell her I was an antique dealer—the

kind who handled Southwest artifacts, so she wouldn't expect
me to know about her valuable pieces.

That made sense to me, my being that, because Henry's
studio-house had a lot of old western stuff, which I'd never
paid much attention to. But it fit in with what we'd just seen,
and it made sense that he'd take an expert along if he was
going to buy something to go with what he had.

"I love the antler mirror," I said, by way of thanking him.
"It's wonderful."

"Next week you can look in it while I work," he said. "Take
your mind off posing."

Then I could see that he was off and painting in his head,
and that made me comfortable again.

. . .

I thought I wouldn't have any trouble with his mother's house,
because I was all dressed up and knew what I was going to
say. But the place knocked me cold. It was all filled with the
heavy old furniture that you see in the kind of places you pay
admission to tour. It looked like the kind of house turned into
a museum that Glenna and Brogan always went to, to show
that they appreciated culture. The kind of house where the
rooms are roped off so that the tourists don't get careless and
stain the upholstery or break a fragile chair leg or chip a piece
of carving off some precious Republic of Texas chair.

It was older than any house I'd ever been in, and had a
lot of features that I knew meant it was expensive but also
knew were the kind of thing that Aunt Glenna would have
covered up as soon as possible.

For instance, the floor was an almost black brown and the
boards were so worn they actually curved down in places, like
in the doorways and on the stairs, from years of people's feet,
but it was polished to shine like a pair of men's shoes and

only had a few rugs scattered on it. And the table where we ate was scarred and nicked and had long dark marks on it, and it was also all waxed and we ate off placemats that left most of the wood bare.

"We're informal here," Mrs. Wozencrantz said while we filled our plates with bubbling hot green enchiladas and carried them into an enormous formal dining room.

She was a skinny straight-up-and-down woman with gray hair and a skimpy gray dress, with the kind of weathered skin that looked like she'd spent most of her life outdoors. Henry's daughter, Karen, was a younger version of the same thing. Although I could tell she was almost my age, she didn't have on any makeup, and with this really tanned skin and light hair and eyelashes, she looked like she would be more at home with horses and dogs than with people.

(The main thing was, she looked unhappy. She looked mad at somebody, maybe her daddy. And I wondered if Henry had ever painted her or if she wished he had. And decided that if I was in her place, I'd be unhappy, too.)

Mrs. Wozencrantz tried to be polite. "Jolene, is it?"

"Yes, ma'am."

"Henry tells me you're an antique dealer."

"I often work with artists," I said, into my part. "They have a good eye."

"Did you enjoy the show?"

"It was interesting." I paused a minute, then added, professionally, "Not everything was in good condition."

"What did you buy, Henry?" she asked him, and he told her about the mirror and named a price so high I almost choked on my food.

"Are you really a dealer?" his daughter asked me.

"More a student of antiques," I lied, which I hated doing. I knew she knew what was going on with me and her daddy, and I wished I could tell her the truth. Kids her age—it hadn't been so long since I was there myself—get lied to all the time by everybody.

"I mean, you're just pretending, aren't you?"

．　．　．

Later, Henry took me on a tour of the house. His mother had gone to her room for a nap, he said, and his daughter was out with some friends. I didn't believe either one of those stories for a minute. I thought they were both behind some thick white wall somewhere, listening to every word we said.

He took me to a room that used to be a back porch and showed me a whole stack of drawings he had done, he said, a long time ago. They were almost like photographs, with every detail lifelike, and some of them looked a little like me. I thought how much I'd hate to have my face painted close-up like that, and was glad that now he had a different style. Being painted like that would be worse than being stark naked in the middle of a busy intersection.

I looked around. It was more of a storage room than a studio, and I could see why he'd got a new place.

He showed me a shelf that contained more drawings, and a bunch of old brushes in jars sitting on the floor, and some boxes of colored chalk he called pastels. He stared at the stuff for a while, then took me back into the main part of the house.

He pointed out the library that had a lot of his mother's art books, and the special seventeenth-century desk where one of his wives used to write letters, and a chair where one of them had sat drinking a lot and watching the sun set. I didn't ask which was the mother of his daughter with the pale eyelashes; I didn't get a feel for either of them, even as ghosts.

We took the antler-framed mirror and let ourselves out the

door. And the main thing I felt—besides that nothing was ever going to happen between Henry and me—was sad, that in the whole huge house full of furniture worth a fortune, all Henry had that belonged to him were a few jars of dried up paintbrushes.

4

"THINK OF a number between two and four," Mom said in my ear.

"Three," I answered stupidly, forgetting that it wasn't her I was supposed to be talking to.

"This isn't *me*," she said. "It's your teacher. Remember? Your nice teacher, Mrs. Evans."

"Okay."

I knew she was going to show up any day. I'd got a card from her, sent to me at Dad's house, saying that she was in New Mexico having a great time at Carlsbad Caverns. That she'd see me in Chillicothe.

Whenever she claimed to be out of the state—which she never was—I knew it meant she was just around the corner. And Chillicothe was another code between us, because it was an old Indian name that meant "the big town where we live." So whenever she wrote me something like that, I knew that any day she'd be showing up to steal me back.

"Three o'clock right before school's out, Jolene, we'll talk about what to do concerning the problem your daddy spoke to me about."

I blinked, trying to keep in my head that she was meaning

to be someone else when she said that. Did she mean she was going to be there at three? But that was time for the bell. I hoped she wasn't going to appear at recess; I'd been through that before.

My dad, whose name is Turk Jackson, had kidnapped me from the playground of my school in Beauregard Heights, and then, again, the same thing, in Honey Grove Hills. (Honey Grove Hills, a name that meant the locusts were supposed to be hanging from honeycombs, was just an area of Texarkana that got its name from a scraggly row of trees the developer had planted at the gates to the subdivision. Its attraction for Mom was that the houses looked so much alike it was all we could do ourselves not to get lost every time we came home from the store.)

The day she called pretending to be the teacher, I was back in San Antonio with the high school kid Dad had hired to look after me until he came home from the office. At that time he was a big-shot salesman for some oil rig equipment company, and wore a suit with a vest to work. The student had been instructed not to let anyone at all talk to me on the phone. Not even if she claimed to be my aunt or my grand-mother.

But Mom had figured that all out. First she'd called the school and said that she was Mr. Jackson's secretary; that he needed my teacher's name so he could call her to talk about the distressing matter of the custody fight. When she had that, she called the house, and asked for Mr. Jackson, explain-ing that she was Jolene's teacher, Mrs. Evans. She said this to the sitter, who was eating the last of a half gallon of Rocky Road ice cream and wishing she was with her boyfriend. When the sitter said he wasn't home, Mom, being the teacher, said that she'd tried his office, and that, oh, dear, maybe she'd better talk directly to the poor little girl.

So that was that. The sitter handed me the phone without

a moment's pause, and turned on the TV. Anyone would have done the same. Mom could sell oil to the Arabs, Uncle Brogan says.

"Three o'clock," I repeated, trying to look like a kid talking to her teacher.

"That's Mrs. Evans talking, not me. That's her saying she's going to have a little chat with you right before the bell rings, see. This is *me*. That was her; now this is me. Nod your head like I'm still her. Are you nodding your head?"

"Yes, ma'am."

"Now, here's what the plan is. I have to get the lay of the land. But you look for me after lunch. There's some spare time after lunch, before the class bell rings. Bathroom time. Wash your hands time. You gobble up your lunch tray—be sure to eat, we aren't stopping till dark, not even a potty stop, so do that, too—and then you look for me. *Generic*. Got that? I'll be there, plain as day, but *Purloin Letter*. You remember what I'm talking about?"

"Yes, ma'am."

"Are you nodding your head? Now the signal will be what I told you. Think of a number between two and four. Got it?"

"Three." I could feel a giggle coming on, but tried to stifle it.

That was one of my mom's oldest jokes. She'd wake me up when we were on the lam, saying, "Think of a number between four and six," if she was letting me know that five A.M. was the time to scoot.

It was good to hear her voice again. Good to have the old jokes back.

The trouble with Dad was that he was a total stranger and we didn't have anything to say because we didn't know the first thing about each other. All he knew for sure was that I was his blood kin. (I imagined he saw me with each red blood corpuscle stamped with the little black letters TURK JACKSON like a bunch of M&Ms.)

So he was always going through this hassle and expense, and taking Tums, and missing sales that should have been in the bag, because he thought it was his fatherly duty to steal me back from Mom.

He'd show up—a balding man with a way of rocking back and forth on his heels—promising, I'm going to give you a normal life. That being the one thing he was sure I was never going to have with Mom.

I guess in the beginning when they were doing the mushy stuff as she calls it, they didn't stop to think that they weren't wanting the same thing at all. Dad for his part when they got married had it in his mind to "take her away" from her gambling family who could hardly keep a roof over their heads, or at least a roof the bank wasn't foreclosing on. So he was always saving money for a rainy day and she was always saying she enjoyed a little shower.

Early on, he set aside a certain amount for a month's rent so they could move out of the room where they were living with my grandparents, but Mom, not liking to see money lying idle, spent it on a set of World Books for me, who, of course, was still too young to read. Then Dad tried another angle and began a big all-out savings program so they could make a down payment on a house of their own. But Mom had no interest in a permanent roof; her idea of romance was to see the sights, to encounter adventure. So when she found the passbook and saw that, by coincidence, the balance was exactly the cost of three seats on the Flying Longhorns' Tour de France, she decided it was the chance of a lifetime, and tucked the tickets in Dad's Christmas stocking: "See *le monde* with Midge and Turk."

That was when they split for good, except for disagreeing over which one of them got me.

. . .

The next day, knowing what was coming, I managed to get out of the house with some money. Dad kept a few tens—I guess all salesmen do that, have stashes of money, of bonuses or percentages or under-the-counter stuff, for dry cleaning the good suit or getting a smart haircut. I took three bills and left him two. That seemed fair; there were more of us.

I was wide awake and excited when we drove to school, and gave Dad, who had fallen asleep in front of the TV the night before, a big kiss when he let me out. He gave me the old pep talk about how everything was all right now. "Normal," he said, sounding tired. "Things are back to normal now."

Sure enough they were.

I ate my lunch in two minutes flat (no great sacrifice if you remember elementary school food) and dumped my tray in the bin. Then I ran down to the restroom for one last visit before I left for the day.

I had no idea what to expect, but I knew Mom would come along. Trying to look casual, like a kid who belonged in the hall, I hurried to the lunchroom again, and then turned and trotted back, both times looking right ahead, not dragging my feet or looking down, ready to say that I was in Mrs. Evans's third grade class and was where I belonged.

The big wall clock was ticking away, and I began to get nervous. I knew once I got in the classroom things were going to close up and there wasn't going to be any easy way for Mom to get me out. Still, I thought maybe she'd barge in saying she was the woman who did free hearing tests (she'd done that before, too) or something like that.

I looked up and down the halls, about to duck back in the

bathroom, when I saw a Terminix man at the far end of the building, holding up three fingers.

Think of a number between—

I ran toward "him" as he lugged his exterminator spray gun toward the outside door, and then we were through it and around the corner of the building and into a car parked in the SCHOOL OFFICIALS ONLY lot and out on the street before I heard the bell ring, the bell that meant lunch was over.

"Mrs. Evans will call Dad when I don't show up," I told Mom.

"I left a note in the school office." She was cool as could be. "Asking them please to excuse Jolene for the rest of the day; that the lawyers on the other side were taking depositions." She looked pleased with herself. "We'll be six hours down the road when your dad gets home from work."

"Where are we going?" I asked, showing her the tens.

"Smart cookie, you are," she said, taking two of them and putting them in her purse. "Very smart cookie. Did you eat?"

"Sure."

"Pee?"

"Sure."

"We're going all the way across the state, right across its equator, its big fat waistband, as far from Honey Grove Hills and old Texarkana as you can get. We're going to El Paso. Next to the border of New Mexico. Nicely adjacent to Diablo, El Capitan, Bright Light, and Frijole. I've got us a swell place lined up in Pass-of-the-Camels Park, which is a suburb so big it looks like L.A. from the air. So big our house has six digits. So big it's impossible not to get lost; we'll need a map to find our door. The houses are built in three styles which repeat, eenie, meenie, miney, down every block for miles and miles and miles. Pass-of-the-Camels Park is the Suburb of Suburbs."

"It'll be good to be home," I said.

5

I FIRST MET L.W. at a party last year.

I was putting one of Mom's rules into effect: check out the terrain before you make your move.

Mostly I was looking for a man, and for sure I wasn't likely to find one the way things were going, not with Brogan and Glenna keeping closer track of me than they did of her prize fur coat. You'd think they'd understand that at eighteen I wasn't a kid at camp having a buddy check every time the whistle blew and a bed inspection at lights out. But I guess they'd got so preoccupied with the idea that I belonged to them until I was twenty-one and that it was their legal job to keep me safe from Mom and Dad until I was of age and all that, that they forgot how it was to be grown and really needing somebody. (Besides, I sometimes thought that Brogan and Glenna had been together since the crib; it was impossible to imagine either one of them being with somebody else, for example.)

I was going to check out the neighborhood, as Mom would say, the neighborhood in this case being a drop-in party. One advantage I had is that in San Antonio you can pretty well figure that you can show up almost anywhere at any function that some program chairman has gone to the trouble to put a notice about in the paper. That you'll be welcome because their main worry is that nobody will show. For instance, if there's a concert or an opening or a play or something arty like that, you know they'll want a crowd; or the same if it's a special interest group (Czech Cooking or Skiing the Alps, for instance), especially if it happens to be downtown but won't appeal to tourists.

So when I saw a notice about a "Texas Exes Thirsty

Thursday, Cash Bar, Nachos and Mariachis," I knew that would be a good gathering for me to get an idea how to pick up somebody in an okay way.

I wore a long poet's skirt, a crinkled blouse made in Taiwan, sandals, with my hair loose. And I knew I was doing fine when nobody gave me a second glance. They all walked past and around me as if I wasn't there, except once when someone in a friendly way asked me for another Margarita and then, seeing her mistake (I didn't have a tray, I wasn't wearing an apron), apologized.

They were all in finance, and went around introducing themselves by their institutions—Smith Barney, Shearson Lehman, Dean Witter—the way I imagined their moms and dads must have mentioned sororities and fraternities.

I got with every sentence they spoke a glimpse of a world where T-bills tumbled and bond prices rose sharply. It was a different world I listened to, getting the cadence of unfamiliar words, catching hold of those that interested me. I stood there with nobody noticing, between someone in convertible securities and someone in mergers and acquisitions, liking the sound of their strange language and storing it for future use.

They were in lovely costume. All of them had shiny bluntcut hair. The boys wore dark silk suits with white shirts; the girls, white suits and dark silk shirts. It was the end of summer.

I was comfortable, standing there in the Zona Rosa cafe, eating nachos and eavesdropping on Texas Exes. I wasn't just someone off the street who'd heard the sounds of a party along the river and decided to drop in—although maybe some of them had. After all, I'd had a year of college; I knew my way around.

When somebody did speak to me, I was surprised. But, when I looked him over, I was glad. He wasn't tall and dark like most of the men, but sort of square, with sandy hair, which was more my type. "Hello," he said, introducing himself right off. "I'm L. W. Dawson."

I noticed his big grin and his cowlick, and decided that at home he'd still be called Buddy by his folks. "Jolene Temple," I told him.

"My Spanish is not so hot," he said, "but I'd have sworn that *Zona Rosa* is border Mexican for red-light district."

I liked his starting right out with that, even if it was something he'd picked up from someone else, which was likely, someone who had made a bilingual pun coming in the door. It wasn't bad, for friendly openers, and besides, I was lonesome and here was someone being friendly.

"Maybe the owners are playing a joke," I said.

He looked at me in a nice way. "You a poet?"

That was good, his picking up on my cues. I gave him a big, warm smile for that, and asked, "How about you?"

He looked at the floor, being modest. "I'm your slow student, I'm afraid. Just about the time I began to get the hang of the market and figure out that someone on his toes could make an unobtrusive dollar buying a little before the facts became common knowledge, the fat hit the fan and insider-trading became a dirty word. Right now I'm getting it the same place everyone else does, from the *Wall Street Journal*. If I don't see it there, I don't know it." At that point he sort of opened up his big palms to indicate disclaimer. At the same time to suggest that maybe he knew a lot more than the bankers standing around us, dreaming of other people's money.

I made a half turn in my skirt, to show I liked his style. "Have you tried the food?"

"It's okay. Back home in Waxahachie, we didn't eat out a lot. They expected me home for dinner every night."

That gave me a good opening, and I took it. "My mom and I," I told him, stepping closer, "used to eat at this diner out on San Pedro. It was run by this big fat man named Pete, who made the best biscuits west of Natchez, and cheese grits with sausage that made your mouth water like a puppy in the summertime. Pete had a sign in his window that said EAT HERE OR WE'LL BOTH STARVE. I guess that sort of became a saying of ours." I glanced around the crowded room, so he'd get the point. "I mean if all you investment people didn't feed off one another—"

L.W. liked that; I could tell he thought it was deep. "That's good," he said. "I see what you mean." He moved in himself and reached for my hand.

I pulled it away, but not in a hurry.

"Maybe we could go somewhere for dinner? It's getting kind of mobbed in here." He slicked down his sandy hair and checked his rep tie.

I was sorry that I couldn't say yes, because I liked him right off and wished I'd met him maybe the second or third time out. But I wasn't sure enough that I could pull it off. I mean, how was I supposed to act once I got to his broker's condo? Was I supposed to know all about his stereo components and VCR and stuff like that? Was I supposed to act like this was something new for me, or that naturally poets did this all the time? Went home with somebody they just met? I couldn't figure it out.

"I have to go," I told him.

"You come to these often?" he asked.

I shook my head. "This is my first Thirsty Thursday."

"Maybe I'll see you next week?"

"Maybe." I looked around. "Are you really a Texas Ex?"

"Class of '84, BBA. But I don't recognize anybody here. I guess at a school with forty thousand students, all of us could have been in the same class and not have known it."

"Maybe we were."

"Not you." He stared at me in a way that made the color rise on my rice-white poet's cheeks. "I'd have noticed you."

"Maybe."

"I mean you stand out." He hesitated, then said what was on his mind. "Some people would be bothered by that."

I knew he meant him. "I'm actually invisible," I told him, at the door.

He laughed.

But I was speaking the truth. It was Mom's rule: the best way to hide is to be conspicuous.

6

OUR RELOCATIONS followed strict guidelines.

First, Mom liked to pick a town on the state line so she could whip across and send misleading postcards home. That was because although we never left the state, Dad never tumbled to that, and was always fuming that she traipsed me all over the country like an Okie Cracker living out of a suitcase.

Second, she liked a big city with a lot of little towns surrounding it, so she could drive Dad and Uncle Brogan nuts trying to decipher postmarks from Bug Tussle, Edhube, New Fulp, Sugar Bottom, when all the time we were in a 'burb in Texarkana, say.

Last, or maybe first, she liked to settle in a nice huge tract with lots of look-alike houses, look-alike driveways, and (she usually managed to lease one, passing herself off as a Head of Household Avon lady) a look-alike car.

So that if the rest of the area were pulling out every day in their Hondas, she was too. Or revving up their Camaros, okay, she liked a good zippy car. This was not for the other eyeballs on the street, of course, who would have accepted a piano teacher driving anything at all, even the sixties peace van she has pictures of herself climbing into. But to make it harder for us to be traced. For instance, if my dad or my uncle was acting on a slim clue, somebody got a postcard and got out the map, then he could hop to the vicinity, but it was a needle in a haystack to find which built-in-1971 ranch-style with the Pontiac in the drive could possibly be ours.

If we'd accumulated a van of furniture (like she had waiting in Pass-of-the-Camels Park), she'd make a great display of moving day, so that the neighbors, peering through their windows, could get a leisurely view of a good sofa being carried in on Mayflower's shoulders, or even a couple of mattresses from U-Haul on ours. When we didn't (such as was the case in Beauregard Heights, where we settled after the airport escape), she rented enough to set up a piano teacher's living room, used her Sears card for guest towels and scented soaps (all little girls who play the piano have to go to the bathroom the minute they walk in the door), and kept the bedroom doors closed.

The next thing was to post notices in the elementary schools. Flyers announcing that those aspiring to be her students must audition as well as bring with them copies of the school's hearing tests. Anyone, she reasoned, who the school thinks has a superior ear, plus who can sit down at the bench and locate the keys without asking half a dozen questions ("Where's the rest of your furniture, Mrs. Temple?"), was going to be a fine student.

From the start she made it clear that hers was not going to be a fly-by-night enterprise for the upwardly mobile, for mothers who wanted piano recitals with froufrou and printed programs (expense and public scrutiny to be at all times avoided). Midge Temple's pupils didn't perform; they studied.

She liked it best when two little girls came to tryouts together, each clutching her credentials and a note from mama. She liked to eye them carefully, eliminate the one likely to tattle at home, choose the other. Thereby intimidating the former and elevating the latter to instant excellence. Thus, before the lessons even began, the contest was over.

That was another of her rules: make your cut *before* the competition starts.

7

A COUPLE OF MONTHS after the Texas Exes party, I went to an opening at the Sun Dog gallery, still hoping to meet someone.

The orange-painted, river-fronting space was packed with pink flowers and a flux of assorted artists. There were painters, all bearded and eager as greyhounds on a leash, dancers with their wonderful thick calves, but mostly the room was filled to overflowing with poets. Dressed in long skirts or unironed pants, gauzy shirts, sandals, all of them had dark eyes (rimmed with kohl or lack of sleep), and all of them had been published: some had done chapbooks, others had been semifinalists for Yale Younger Poet.

I drank white wine and listened to the litany of small magazines that had held their lines: *Milkweed, Loonfeather, Runestone, Blue Unicorn.*

I wore a dark silk suit with a white crepe shirt and my blunt-cut dark hair shone. In my free hand, I carried a briefcase, and on the wrist of the same hand wore a large black watch, to indicate that I was a person who kept her appointments.

Hearing the poets' speech fall into rhymed lines or find its natural meter, I was also searching the crowd for a painter. I was longing for a man, and had decided that a painter might like someone willing to pick up the tab.

I had narrowed my choice to two, having first ruled out the ones who'd been pressured to come—a friend's brother, the owner's nephew—those putting in an appearance, those clearly only passing through the klieg-lit, well-shadowed place. The pair who remained, both in faded blue work shirts, seemed to me equally attractive, likely to shed equal warmth in bed.

Putting Mom's rule into effect, I decided to make my cut before the fact.

Both painters hovered. I kept my voice low, answering their questions about my work in a pleasant voice. "I'm your slow student, I'm afraid." I looked at the floor. "Just about the time I began to get the hang of the market and figure that someone on her toes could make an unobtrusive dollar buying a little before the facts became common knowledge, the fat hit the fan and insider-trading became a dirty word. Right now I'm getting my information the same place everyone else does, the *Wall Street Journal*. If I don't see it there, I don't know it."

The one a little older, in the more weathered work shirt, with an interesting face and deep-set eyes, bent down slightly to look at my reptile shoes. Wondering if he was counting cost or had a sudden longing to see my foot out of its pump, I made my choice.

Slipping a hand through his arm, I presented myself. "I'm Jolene Temple."

"Henry Wozencrantz." His voice was expectant. He seemed to think I'd recognize the name.

"My feet hurt," I confessed. "Do you live nearby?"

The other painter, not selected, wandered off across the orange-tile floor to get himself another drink.

. . .

At that precise moment, I heard a familiar voice. Turning halfway, in order not to shift my instep, I saw L.W., in unpressed pants and an Indian shirt. He wore blue-tinted glasses and no socks.

"All of us trying to sell our poems to one another," he was saying, "reminds me of a story—"

"Excuse me for a moment," I said to the painter. "I think I was in school with that boy."

"Back home in Waxahachie," L.W. told his semicircle of admirers, "my dad and I used to eat at this diner. It was run by a fat man named Pete who made the best biscuits west of Natchez, and cheese grits with sausage that made your mouth water like a puppy in the summertime. Pete had this sign in his window that said EAT HERE OR WE'LL BOTH STARVE." He paused to let that sink in. Glancing up, his eyes tripped over my face. "If we don't all read one another's work—"

"Hello," I said.

"Jolene. It's you." He pulled me off to one side.

"The same."

"Not quite," he observed.

"You either."

"I guess you're an actor, too."

I nodded, although without a lot of conviction.

"You did a great poet at the Zona Rosa," he said sincerely.

"Thanks. You were good, too, your broker."

"I was nervous."

"It didn't show."

"It was a new approach for me." He looked admiring.

"What was?"

"The way you did, standing out from the crowd."

"It's a lot harder your way, blending in." There were a dozen things I wanted to ask him. Had he been in real plays? Did he take class? What was he doing at the opening of the Sun Dog? Did he really think my poet was good? . . . I looked at his broad face, his good Buddy disposition, and wished we had met some other way.

"I thought I saw you," he said, "over there. But I wasn't sure."

"Do you really live in Waxahachie?"

"No. I live right here in San Antonio with my folks, same house where I've lived all my life."

"Did you know Waxahachie is an Indian word meaning"—I grinned at him—"cow chip?"

"You're kidding." He looked impressed at my knowledge. "Is there really a diner on San Pedro?"

"I never looked."

"We could find out; I live near there." He took my hand. I hesitated, because I liked him a lot. "I can't."

"Are you going home with that painter?"

"I guess so."

"Why?"

"Why that one?" I was about to explain Mom's rule. "You know—"

"I'm lonesome."

"There's me."

"But you aren't *you*. I mean, don't you see, I'm not *me*, either. The painter is the painter all the time."

"If you say so." He looked doubtful.

"Oh, L.W., don't you see? Actors meet only on the stage."

8

*O*N DECEMBER I got cold feet.

Although my Reeboks were getting wet in an unexpected downpour, I admitted the real cause was an attack of stage fright in the jingle-bell, Salvation Army, Santa Claus time of year.

During the first part of the semester when our wild-haired, old, and famous teacher had given us parts to read aloud, I'd liked acting class a lot. It had felt familiar, as if Mom had branched out into further efforts at disguise. As if, reading some other character's part, I'd vanish before their eyes, become a four-year-old Sonny, and other designated roles.

But then last week she had sprung improvisation on us. And suddenly there were all the rest of the kids wrestling their smiles to the floor, acting out the color blue, turning into a biscuit rising.

The famous teacher got mad at me. First she'd been disappointed, then surprised, and then she got mad. "Loosen up, Jolene," she commanded, but her words only hastened me into a state of panic.

This week, I got to class early, me and half a dozen other students. We were in leotards, with cotton sweaters and slightly sweaty faces from all our outside vests and jackets. Standing around like extras in the big San Antonio College studio, we looked as if we'd all tried out for the role of beginning student and hadn't yet heard who'd got the part.

Every time the door opened, letting in chill wet air and fresh eager actors, I caught my breath and turned to stare. But that was just wishful thinking: L.W. wouldn't be showing up, or else he'd have been coming all along.

As the teacher began to talk, I tensed my legs, pulled up

on my toes, let my shoulders go limp. Trying to stay calm, I stretched and attended. "Thespians on the boards," she told us, "must produce a chemistry between them. They must master the Theater of the Impromptu."

She looked straight at me. "Jolene? Show us," she demanded. "Be something with wheels."

I stared at her but couldn't move. My mouth went dry as sawdust.

All around me everyone was itching to perform, rotating with longing to be a bicycle, a motorcycle, a velocipede.

But not I. I froze up solid as a block of ice. I couldn't do it. I couldn't get up there in front of them and make it up by myself—turn it on from the inside out. I kept looking around, panicked, waiting for instructions. Waiting for someone to say, "Jolene, are you listening?" to say, "Now here's what we're going to do," but nobody did.

Grabbing my sweater I bolted for the door.

Outside in the cold, I warmed myself by imagining a family around a table in some place like Beauregard Heights, a family with grandparents whose feet barely touched the floor, presiding over their daughters and sons and the children of their daughters and sons. There was a pine tree in the parlor of the house, and another tree, a spreading spruce, in the kitchen. Both hung heavy with ornaments and icicles, their branches hiding packages wrapped and stacked.

I imagined another family up the road in Waxahachie, gathered around a fir with that just-cut smell, while a grandfather said the blessing and a grandmother added up who was there.

I felt an instant relief; I had other options.

I didn't have to stay in class. I could be a painter's model.

9

$\mathcal{T}$HE FIRST TIME I showed up to pose for Henry, I was scared. The way you would be if you were going to take your clothes off for a centerfold spread or something. I could imagine somebody in the oil business, jerking off in his motel room, seeing me and calling up Uncle Brogan. "Hey, Brog, I don't know how to mention this, buddy, but I'm holding here in my left hand . . ." The worst.

But that first afternoon, while I still had on my jeans, Henry made me see that it was not going to be like that. He got out some slides of his work to show me, because he said that naturally artists never kept their pictures around the studio. That that was inviting theft, and anyway, his agent always wanted them the minute he finished to place in galleries or whatever he did with them. That what artists had around were slides of their work, in case they needed to send a museum something to look at, for a show or a jury prize or something like that.

I was nervous about his showing them to me, that he was going to want me to say something about his pictures. I was afraid he was going to expect me to know the art words to use, maybe ask him something like, Isn't that impressionism? or Don't they call that abstract art? I was afraid he was going to want me to make the comments that somebody who knew what they were seeing would make. And I wished I'd taken an art history course, so I could say that his pictures reminded me of, and give a name, which, even if it wasn't the right thing to be reminded of, was at least having some idea. But I didn't know anything. Art is not a major concern of Brogan and Glenna's. Or Mom's either. So I was scared and about ready to say, Don't go to all that trouble, really, never mind, when he said, "Look here, Jolene. Take a look." And he held these slides up to the light so I could see them. (They were in color, meaning the photos, since naturally the paintings were, if that's what you call it.)

I squinted and looked at what seemed to me to be a great big sand dune, maybe one of the type used in films, that camels ride across while the sun is about to fry them and the heavy music is playing. "That's a shoulder," Henry said. "Look at this." Then he showed me another that was some sort of big bridge or half a donut, because it was round and light at the top, then dark at the bottom like an open place or a hole. It looked beautiful, which is a strange thing to say about something like that, but it did. "That's a kneecap," he said.

Then he put the slides away and talked a little bit about the way he puts paint on canvas, and all the time I was not relaxing totally—in case there was going to be some kind of quiz afterwards, to see if I'd understood what he said or to see if I was paying attention. But then when he got ready for me to pose, it was all right. Because that's when I saw that all the painting he does is sort of in his head, and that whatever he puts in his pictures while he's working is not anything that anybody can recognize. And that all he wants from me is for me to hold still and concentrate, and I didn't mind learning to do that.

"I'm going to paint your breasts with the artificial hand between them," he said that first day, arranging me with a sheet tied to keep the bottom of me covered, so I wouldn't distract him by being too nervous. "They're too big. I'm going to do them like two green grapes. Just the green grapes with the, ummm, wrist."

I shut my eyes and tried to imagine something as big as a wall with two green ovals and a sort of tree trunk (the wrist) in the middle. I liked that, and relaxed some.

After a while he said, "They're too small. I want something heavy. Something with veins. I'm going to do them like cantaloupe. With only—hold it lower, lower—only the fingers, the index finger." And I imagined the rind of melons with something joined and pointed (the finger) crawling up between them. And that was when I got it right, concentrating on holding it.

The smooth porcelain felt, that first time, as if the little girl's hand had been torn loose at the wrist trying to break away. As if somebody had held on to the owner and wouldn't let her go, so she pulled loose and left her hand, the way animals, tearing themselves out of traps, leave a paw behind.

10

TODAY, HENRY SAYS I can select another hand. This is because he's so pleased still, about the spilled flowers and the tablecloth business.

He hasn't been in the mood to do it sitting up any more, so he's been trying something new. Today he got the idea he'd like me standing up, bending over, and first he tried it with me leaning over the back of a chair, with my panties at my feet. Then he got me to stand by this table where he puts stuff like bowls of fruit or vases of flowers, things that other artists might paint, still lifes, but he doesn't do that. He just keeps the table with something arranged on it, as a sort of joke for himself.

Anyway, he had me leave on my skirt and lean across the table, and then he took his arm and knocked over the silver vase with some daisies in it, and the water dripped on the

floor and he pushed my skirt up and the top of me was lying
face down, and he thought that was great. He did it a couple
more times. Each time starting with the vase full and sitting
up there, and me in this skirt, and then pulling up my skirt
and knocking over the vase. It made him come real fast, but
it also made him laugh at the same time. Because of course
he was painting in his head.

. . .

He knows I love to look at the hands, but usually he won't let
me, because, he says, he has memories about them, and that
I let the memories out—Pandora's Box—and that gets in the
way of his working.

The history of the hands is that his uncle was a famous
photographer, and when Henry was a young boy, maybe about
fourteen, old enough to be thinking about doing it, his uncle
had this mistress who'd lost a hand. (He always says she was
his uncle's mistress, but since his uncle never married, I don't
think that's the right word. More likely, she was his uncle's
girlfriend.) Anyway, the uncle would have the black cloth over
his head that old photographers used, and she would stand
there posing in a black cape, sort of like she belonged a hundred years ago in Paris, Henry says. And she had these big
dark eyes and all this long dark hair. (At first he said I looked
just like her, but then he took that back.)

She had lost a hand in an accident—someone closed a car
door on it when she was a kid. She didn't really live, naturally,
in Paris before cars, but in some ordinary place like Beauregard Heights, where she was just another little kid. She'd had
all these artificial hands made for her as she grew up. The
ones that have the fingers curving and fixed like a doll's, made
of fine china. Then there are the later ones, that have a spring
inside so that you can open and close them like a clamp.

These are made of heavy steel and each has on a tight glove of what seems like real skin. That's so you can get them to match the color of your own, Henry says. The way dentists have false-teeth chips to match your own teeth. What is strange about these is that the glove, the covering, comes way up over the wrist. That's because it's made to slip over the end of your real arm so that it will look real, too.

I could look at the hands forever. My favorite, the one I picked first, the one I've been holding when I pose, was the very first, the oldest. It's a porcelain one, very dainty looking, with slightly spread fingers and the palest pink nails painted on.

When Henry first opened the drawer and let me see the whole collection, I could hardly stand it. I don't know why I love them so much, or why it makes me so happy to look at them, touch them. It sounds creepy, but the way some little girls play with dolls, I bet I could play with the hands all day long. I'd like to take them all out and arrange them on the bed in rows. And hold each one up to a sleeve, and sort of grow her up. Does that make sense? Probably it sounds weird. But some things you think would sound weird to tell don't seem that way at all when you do them. It feels as if it would be the most natural thing in all the world, to get the hands out and play with them.

. . .

"I'm going to sit you down today," Henry says, "so take your pick. Something different. My uncle always chose for her. He didn't want the hand to show; just the fingers, from under the cape. It was his private joke. You can't tell it in his photographs of her—and he did a whole collection, two shows— that she has anything wrong. They made him famous; and no one spotted the hand."

(I sometimes try to imagine this business about what people mean when they say *famous*—his uncle, my drama teacher with the wild hair. Exactly what it is they're talking about. Whether they're saying they could walk down the street of any city and that everyone would turn to look at them, the way you would if somebody like Michael Jackson passed you. Or if it only means that they get written up in places that only other people who do the same thing know about. For instance, in books about acting, or photography magazines. Maybe it means that everybody moves out of the way when you come in a room; that they all stare at you. That kind of famous would be embarrassing. I wouldn't think you'd brag about that.)

Henry says he used to come and stand and watch his uncle shoot his mistress for hours. That he was in love with her, or thought he was, the way a fourteen-year-old boy would be. That he would have given anything in the world to have sex with her. That she was very beautiful but that she never looked at him—only at his uncle.

He shakes the drawer slightly, ready to start. "Go on, pick one," he says.

I select one of the grown-up hands, with its smooth fingernails complete with half moons, its curved, shaped fingertips, its tight flesh slipped over cold, spring-held metal.

He sits me on the couch and takes off the sheet. I try to put my mind on posing. He has me hold the hand between my legs, and he spreads them so that the hand is right on top of the hair down there. That actually feels okay. I don't need to distract myself with the antler mirror any more, or even to have the sheet tied around my hips. I can put my posing on automatic.

I lean back and get ready to concentrate on how it will look. The fingers spread as big as fence posts, poked in the black grass between two huge white sand dunes, on a bare part of the beach.

But then Henry decides he's going to put the necklace on me. "You'll feel dressed," he says, laughing. And I can tell that he's already through painting and has moved on to sex in his head.

So I let him put the flat turquoise and silver necklace around my throat, and I do feel more dressed, and then I laugh, too.

11

"YOU THINK about yourself a certain way long enough, that's the way you get to be." Uncle Brogan is talking about the state of Texas.

"You think about yourself a certain way long enough, you get delusions." Aunt Glenna Rose is talking about Brogan's scheme for a cocktail party for his cellular car phone cronies at the La Fonda Sur Rosa Motel—which everybody in the city calls the Sub Rosa.

I'm in the middle between them, listening, because they like to have a third-party opinion. That's one of the reasons they decided to take me in when everybody got tired of Mom and Dad stealing me back and forth all the time.

We're on the patio, where we sit every Sunday morning, no matter whether it's baking hot in the summer or crisp and bright blue, like now, at the end of winter. They're in their pink sweat suits, having Snappy Tom and feeling fit because they're not drinking Bloody Marys.

"Look at the mess Texas is in. Here you've got the Energy Department of the federal government deciding to make a toxic dump instead of wheat fields out of Deaf Smith County, so all the Panhandle's in an uproar.

"You've got the red tide infestation poisoning the entire shrimp and oyster industry from the mouth of the Colorado to the Mexican border, for God's sake, ten thousand bloated fish on Gulf of Mexico tourist beaches. And our very own trees, our own Oldest Plants in the South trees, are suffering from the Texas Live Oak Decline disease.

"Plus, doesn't this take the cake, some bunch of dropout indigents have dug up our one-hundred-million-year-old dinosaur tracks right up the road here on farm-to-market 1826, stolen them right out of the ground.

"And those are just the trivial complaints; the mosquito bites. I'm not even mentioning that thirty-three thousand and nine hundred individuals, that's neighbors and cousins and old buddies from junior high, have filed for the big Chapter Eleven."

"Are you counting us?" Glenna Rose is spreading out a stack of plastic credit cards on the wrought iron table.

"Think about it. When you were growing up, bankrupt was what you went when you lost your houses on Boardwalk. It wasn't something happened to real people. It's an epidemic. Chapter Eleven is spreading down every street. I bet we have at least two folks right here in our very own neighborhood, right here off North New Braunfels, who have declared bankruptcy this very week."

"Hmmm." Glenna makes one row of MasterCards and a second row of Visas.

"Texas," Brogan says, "Texas, the state of Texas, is like a fat kid with pimples who can't get a date for Saturday night. Last year, the year before, he could have had anybody including your head cheerleader. Now he can't even get a yes from a barking dog."

"Brogan, listen to these prices." Aunt Glenna is reading

off the room service menu sent out by the motel along with the confirmation of their suite. "I'm reading to you. Oysters Rockefeller. *Bienville* or *Casino.*" She uses a heavy French accent.

"Forget oysters at this point, hon. You've got some vested interests invited who aren't going to want to be reminded of the trouble in the coastal waters."

"Canton ribletts, sweet and sour dipping sauce. One hundred eighty-five an order. Fenneled sausage in crust, the same. That's just snacks, Brogan. Snacks. Your basic cheese and crackers—Jarlsberg, Camembert, Boursin—is ninety-five. One order of nachos. I'm talking about a tiny little plate of nachos, period, is twelve bucks. Plus the bar. Look at this." She holds up a glossy laminated list headed FULL BAR. "We're not having these clients of yours spending an evening with Seven-Up. Full bar, it says, six hundred sixty-seven, and it's a bunch of junk. I mean who drinks this stuff? Dewar's? Bacardi? Sweet Vermouth? They must be some kind of chain-mentality motel, thinking they've got folks from Detroit or something. I mean it looks"—she works on a piece of paper with a ball point—"it looks like we're talking about five a bottle per Lone Star and about eighty dollars a bottle for Jack Daniel's by the time they get through adding on for the ice and glasses and service. For those prices we could have it at your five-star restaurant out on Broadway. We could have it at *Lou Tess!*"

She turns to me for a third opinion. "Jolene, honey, do you understand why we have to have this party at the Sub Rosa? Why we can't have it here at our own house?"

Brogan answers her before I can say a word. (That's one reason I like to be around them a lot; most of the time they don't even know I'm here.)

"I'll tell you why. We're going to get them to thinking like Texans again, that's why. Get them to thinking like boys who can get any Saturday night date in the whole damn school.

Give them back a good view of themselves. Give these ranchers and business types a party like in the good old days, with ice sculptures and Mr. Jack on the rocks, and a mountain of little pink crawdaddies on toothpicks, and ribs enough to look like the remains of the Alamo.

"We're going to turn them around. Do you get the idea? Glenna? Jolene, tell her what the message is, can't you? You young folks understand the concept of the loss leader."

"I figure"—Aunt Glenna Rose is adding up sums of money, this time having to do with credit cards—"we got maybe, just outside maybe, about one hundred fifty dollars' worth of credit here before me. That is not enough to serve your cellular transceiver preferential customers an order of French fries. Not to mention the drop-ins and the word-of-mouths and the friends of friends."

"Look what I have here," Brogan announces. He's pacing back and forth, looking red in the face but healthy. He's sucking in his stomach and every once in a while stops to do deep knee bends or arm swings. Now he is waving something in the air.

"What's that?" she says.

"It happens to be a check for four hundred and twenty-five dollars made out to yours truly, that's what." He slaps it down on the table in front of her. "A consolidation loan. I got myself a consolidation loan."

Glenna Rose's soft voice rises to a shriek. "Brogan Temple, I'm looking at us owing twenty-four thousand dollars basic minimum, and twenty-four hundred just to keep them from cutting off our credit, minimum basic, and you're planning this humongous party with *four hundred twenty-five dollars?*"

Brogan drops into the chair next to her. "Hon, you got to have cash. You got to have cash for the fellow who parks your cars and the one that sets up the bar and the one that does a little extra number on not noticing all the liquor you brought in yourself. This is essential cash flow, Glenna. You're looking at the cash flow that makes this possible.

"The motel, they're going to take our card. They're in the business of taking anybody's card because they've got two hundred rooms to rent out every night, and they know if they turn away everybody who's extended himself a little on his credit that they'll be the ones claiming Chapter Eleven by the end of the week."

He bends down close to her face and gives her a kiss on the ear. "What we needed was the twenties. You got to have a pocket full of twenties. Clients, they see you got loose twenties, when they're taking out bank loans to pick up the dry cleaning and vaccinate the baby, they get the idea you're rich. If you're rich, and you're in the business of selling cellular automobile phones, then maybe they get the idea to expand the number of car phones they've got, and then they'll be rich, too. While their brothers-in-law are having to sneak across the state line to file their Elevenses in Louisiana."

Glenna flicks through the cards. "I should have kept my own name."

"You didn't have an own name."

"I did so."

"Besides, what's the point of an own name in a community-property state? You got homestead. We file a Chapter Eleven you get the homestead and they can't take it away from you."

"Honest?" Glenna Rose likes their great big sprawling gray and pink ranch-style a lot.

"You bet. But that is not going to be the case. Let me read you this little item here." Brogan takes a newspaper clipping out of his attaché case on the empty chair. "This is the photo of a man in the little state of New Jersey buying two hundred thousand pounds of cocoa for his business. He's driving, see here, down the Garden State Parkway, talking into his cellular, on his way to the headquarters of Nabisco to negotiate the cocoa powder for a secret project. This is such hot news, this man's call—you have to understand we're talking East Coast now—that it was on the front page of the paper. It is such hot news that this entrepreneur, this cookie king, is ordering his cocoa powder, discussing his top secret recipe, because he's doing it on a *car phone*."

"Where'd you get this?"

"The company sent it around. Front page, third section, *New York Big Times*."

"That looks like a Lincoln he's driving." Glenna squints at the grainy heavyset man in the clipping, then at his car.

"Good P.R. Now, what are our ranchers going to think? That they should give up? That they should quit? Just because the price of oil has dropped to the height of a gopher's behind? Because their cattle are going to be munching nuclear wastes instead of alfalfa? Because half the fish in the Gulf of Mexico are floating face up? When this cookie cutter has got his picture in the center of the page, smuggling in secrets for a new batch of chocolate chips? Making money hand over fist? They're going to see this—I've got a flyer being printed up right this very minute—and ask themselves why aren't they out there drumming up business. That's what they'll be asking. Are they quitters, are they whiners, are they going to let East Coast cocoa brokers get it all? That's what they're going to be asking."

Glenna turns to me. "Honey, I'll need your help."

"All right."

"I mean we'll need a pretty girl." She stacks the credit cards and puts a rubber band around all but one of them. "I mean you can dress up and pass the cheese or something."

"Okay."

Glenna purses her mouth. Realizing she's making wrinkles, she takes a finger and smooths the lines on her forehead. "When I was growing up, my mom thought we were having a party when she baked Mamie Eisenhower's pumpkin pie."

"Your mom . . ." Brogan makes a face.

"At least *my* mom didn't lose her house in a bingo game every other week."

"Shush."

"Jolene . . ." Glenna is trying to figure out how to say something to me.

I'm trying to figure out what it is, and if it's something I can do. I owe her a lot. She was the one who decided that she and Brogan should take me. She was the one always at home that had to get the phone and hear my mom and dad screaming that I'd been kidnapped right off the playground, right out of the hall, from Sunday School, from a birthday party. She was the one nice enough to take me in six years ago, give me this nice safe place here with her and Brogan, make clear to Mom and Dad that these premises were definitely off-limits to them until I reached the age of twenty-one. That if they came creeping around, hanging out in the hedges, peeping in the windows, ready to pounce and drag me back when somebody's back was turned the way they liked to do, that they'd have her, Glenna Rose Temple, right arm of the law, to personally answer to. Like I say, I owe her a lot.

"Honey," she says again, smoothing at her wrinkles, "is there something else we can say you do? I mean there's nothing wrong with actress, I mean if you were. If you were somebody in the movies, if you were Cissy Spacek or something. But these clients just don't get the right idea when you say *actress*. It sounds, I don't know—but if you could think of something else?" She looks at me, hopeful, wanting to be sure she hasn't hurt my feelings. "I don't guess there's anything wrong with just telling them you're a student in college. That's something to be proud about."

This seems to me the perfect time to tell her the news. "Well, actually, I'm not right now." I scoot my chair across the brick patio closer to hers. "I didn't want to tell you all— I was afraid you'd be mad because I wasted that tuition money. But I didn't see a future for myself, like you say, in films. So I've got a job, for now, as a model."

"A model?" Glenna Rose brightens up. "That's great. Did you hear that, Brogan? Jolene is a *model.*"

"Is that so?" He comes over and looks at me to see how he should take the idea. "I thought you had to be skin and bones."

"Not any more. They like you natural now." I try not to imagine myself in Henry's studio when I say that.

"I thought you had to be six foot tall?"

"That's high fashion."

"*Hot coat-ture,*" Aunt Glenna says. "Paris. You're talking Paris, Brogan, skin and bones. Here, people like to see what looks good on someone like them." She turns to me. "Well, that's swell, honey. And you should have told us right off. Don't worry about the money. I'll get the doctor to write a note and say you had mono and you'll get every dime back. You'll get your tuition back and be making money besides."

"Maybe she'll pay for the party," Brogan kids. He pours himself a Snappy Tom, looking, on balance, pleased at this development.

And for the millionth time I think how lucky I am to be living with them.

For one thing, neither Mom nor Dad would have let my story go for one single minute without getting to the bottom of it.

12

A WEEK AFTER the planning session, I get a postcard from Mom.

It says:

J——

I'm in Tennessee, having a great time finding out how the natives like all those Japanese auto plants.

See you in Chillicothe.

Love,
M——

13

IT'S CREEPY, the way Mom and Dad always make their moves at the same time, as if they were connected by telepathy.

The day after I get the card from Mom, which I don't show around, Brogan gets a letter from Dad, which he does. Dad says he might be in the vicinity in the near future, that he might stop by to look in on his "must be nearly grown by now" daughter.

I can't figure out this sudden interest on their parts. It's been six years since I even set eyes on either one of them. What do they want with me now?

Brogan and Glenna tell me not to worry; that I am absolutely lead-pipe safe from Mom and Dad. Brogan says that he and Glenna got a quit-claim to me—and then he stops and explains that that's a term used in the oil business about leases on the back forty but that he means Mom and Dad don't have any more right to come sniffing around me like hound dogs. Besides, he says, the statute of limitations has run out. Imagine, he jokes, if parents could come back forty years down the road and yank you back.

To which Glenna asks, And what does he think his are doing?

But I don't wholly believe what he says, because I've got fear running up and down my backbone with those two letters popping up out of the blue, and I don't have the confidence that he does that Mom and Dad aren't up to their old tricks again. Sometimes when you've been feeling more or less safe and then something comes along and pulls that feeling out from under your feet, it's almost worse than it was before. I mean in the old days, when I was a kid, I sort of got used to it. It became almost a game: hightailing it out of this place; hunkering down out of sight in that one. But now I don't think I could start all that up again. Or, rather, starting it all up again is too truly awful to think about.

But it isn't until I get up in the middle of the night, not sleeping too well, to get a drink of water, that I get some idea of what might be behind my sudden popularity. Behind Mom and Dad suddenly deciding that I'm up for grabs again.

.   .   .

"I think this model business is okay," Brogan says, in a worried hoarse whisper, "but there are a bunch of consequences."

"Like what?" Glenna sounds half asleep.

"It upsets the applecart, taxwise."

"How's that?" She doesn't sound as sleepy.

"You can't claim a dependent who's nineteen unless she's in school full time and making peanuts a year. You follow? Her being a kid and in school and not working we had every angle covered. Now, I don't know. There goes nineteen hundred bucks for a dependent."

"You think that's why that lunk got in touch? He needs the extra cash? Would he go through all that again to get nineteen hundred off his taxes?"

"Would Turk Jackson sell his mother for five dollars? Besides, times are tough. With the whole state claiming Chapter Eleven, how many folks are buying drilling-rig parts for wells they've closed?"

"I see what you mean."

"Plus having her back would give him Head of Household. And if he doesn't earn any more than my sister, he can also get Earned Income Credit."

"You think Midge will show up, too?"

"How many people are shelling out these days for piano lessons do you imagine?"

"Oh, hon."

"I'm not meaning to worry you. That's a swell girl in there. I'm not giving her up. I just had this thought in the back of my head, when she said she'd got this modeling job."

"How would the feds know?"

"They got eyes. They got eyes with computers."

"Then she can just enroll and take something. How do you know that she's making money anyway? Maybe she's doing tearoom modeling for department stores. Maybe she gets minimum wage. What's that, about a dollar seventy-five?"

"Dating yourself, baby. How about three thirty-five."

"No kidding? Is it? Let's ask her."

"Ask her what?"

"What she makes."

"That's her business."

"She could pay us rent."

"Forget that idea. I only mentioned it. I got dollars on the brain these days."

"I bet that's why he wrote. That big lout gives me the creeps."

Silence. Then, "Brogan?"

"What?"

"Do you think maybe we've protected her too much?"

"Protected her? Too much?"

"You know, sort of kept her close to home, put a wall around her, trying to make sure that nobody could come take her away."

"There's no such thing as protecting girls too much, so put that idea out of your mind. It's a contradiction."

Everything is quiet, and then Glenna says, "Brogan?"

"No more tonight. Come on. Forget it for now. We got enough on our minds."

"Brogan?"

"All right, what?"

"Should I wear my coat?"

"Should you wear your coat?"

"You know, my *Joie de Beavre*, my genuine full-skin dyed beaver with fox shawl collar. To the customers' party."

"You bet. Greet them at the door. Tell them you ordered it over the cellular from your Lincoln Continental. We'll run the air conditioning all evening."

"You're sweet, you know?"

"That's me."

14

I DECIDE that maybe I should look up L. W. Dawson.

That maybe I was in too big a hurry to say it wouldn't work out for us.

If he hadn't been in the phone book, I wouldn't have worried. Years with Mom and Dad had taught me how to find any needle in any haystack. I had out my city map—remembering that he said he lived near San Pedro—and I filled up the old Buick that Brogan and Glenna had given me when I first got my license (back when it was only a ten-year-old car, the kind you'd give away in those days when the Blue Book price was about fifty dollars and everybody had money then and was getting excited about imports).

On the map there were about four different areas in that general part of town, residential areas. Each with a little cluster of houses—Anglo beginning to mix down; Mexican beginning to mix up. Each the kind of neighborhood where you can imagine behind every door somebody retired peering out between the department-store curtains at who is moving in next door and getting ready for the offensive or the defensive, depending on their personality.

In other words, the kind of neighborhood I like a lot. The kind we never lived in, even in the early days, because Mom figured there wasn't much demand for piano teachers among the retired, and the young in such areas were too busy moving up or moving down to be bothered with such refinements. But, principally, because she liked us to be lost in the crowd, and each of these was the type of neighborhood where having a one-of-a-kind house was the rule. So if somebody was coming over to see you, you'd be able to mention, "It's the pink

stucco with the Spanish tiles," or "It's the Tudor with the
stone collie in the front." And even your acquaintances would
never need to know your house number, and your real friends
wouldn't even know the street name. They'd just know to
turn off San Pedro at the green house with the fifteen hanging ferns on the porch, then turn right by the yard with the
dozen clay ducks on a painted pond, and then yours would
be the third house, the peach one with the twenty-three bird
feeders, each a careful replica of the White House.

I was going to look up all the Dawsons one by one, picking
first the subdivision whose streets ended in -*wood* (because I
liked the sound of those best), and then going on to those
with -*hurst*, and finally, a newer one, not as old and settled,
an area where the streets had the names of Texas flowers
(Bluebonnet, Paint Brush).

If I didn't find L.W. that way, I had other tricks up my
sleeve. I won't go into all of them, but one thing you can
do—I know because Dad was always doing it—when people
are hiding out is you can go to the elementary school and find
out if there is an L. W. Dawson enrolled, or, in this case, if
there ever was one. You can say you're his long-lost sister,
that's what I was going to use, or you have bad news about
the little girl's grandmother, that was Dad's line, and then
they'll look it up for you every time. School people are proud
whenever they can produce definite information on three-by-
five cards for you, so they never pursue why you're asking.
That way, if L.W. lived with some folks named Smith, of
which there are pages and pages, or Rodriguez, of which there
are even more pages, then I could still find the address where
he'd lived. Then, if he'd moved, well, that begins to take time,
but you get the idea how it goes. Because somewhere in there,
to enroll in school you've got to show a birth certificate, so
the real name gets written down, and once you're written
down in a school you're there forever.

(And I guess Jolene Temple/Jackson is enrolled in at least a dozen.)

But in this case it was as easy as opening the phone book— by which fact I got the information that his folks had nothing to hide and never had. There was an L. W. Dawson on Rosewood and also a Lenox Worth Dawson at the same address. I liked that. It made me wonder whether he was the one who was called "L.W." at home, or if the son used those old names and the daddy got the initials.

I told myself I ought to call first. What if he wasn't there? What if he was but it was an awkward time for me to show up?

But I knew that to pretend to be weighing the options was an exercise in talking to myself. Because I never, and I am never in my life going to, pick up the phone unless somebody is standing by me and I can't get out of it. (Mom and Dad used to make me be the one to place calls, be the one to get in touch with Brogan and Glenna, or the bank, or the car lease place.) The reason is that you are without any disguise on the phone.

They can't see if you are in a poet's skirt or a broker's suit or if you are someone they're supposed to know. All you've got is your voice. And I know those funny scenes in films when people play at being different people on the phone, using different voices—or they're not being funny, they're being killers—but the point is that you, who are watching the film, know who they really are and what is happening. You can pretend to be the person being fooled, but you're not being fooled. And you're not in real life being the one trying to lie and having only your voice to do it with.

Plus every time the phone rang when I was a kid, it was usually Mom or Dad, the one who didn't have me, pretending to be someone she wasn't or he wasn't, to find out if I was there, or where I was. And I always got this sinking feeling when people said they were the school principal or the dentist—because I knew one of them was on my trail again.

The point is that to me the telephone is an instrument for lying—and I can't imagine that people who aren't would want to talk on it if they could help it. (It proves my point that right this minute Brogan is calling up his clients about the big March 2 Texas Independence Day Bash, at La Fonda Sur Rosa, telling them that the economy is turning around, that if they'll only buy even more phones than the ones they already have, so they don't even own a car without a phone, then they'll all be rich as *Creases*, as Brogan always pronounces it.)

. . .

So I head for Rosewood, which runs right into San Pedro. And in a way I'm disappointed: it's no challenge at all. And I have to smile to myself, as if I were missing the old days. As if I were enjoying the shoe being on the other foot, and me being the one looking for someone for a change.

That makes me laugh a little, and I decide that if somebody who looks all wrong answers the door—Mrs. Lenox Worth, or L.W. Senior—then I can pretend I'm the Avon lady. And thinking about that brings Mom back, so I'm not quite smiling any more by the time I pull up in front of the Dawsons' house and see that their name is written on the mailbox in metal script made to look like rope. Like a lariat painted copper on the cream-colored box. "Just look for the mailbox"—that's what you'd say if you lived in their house and weren't hiding out from anyone.

When I ring the bell, L.W. himself answers the door (which has a shellacked rope lassoed around it, too), and I'm really glad to see him. That's how L.W. makes me feel.

"Jolene." He looks knocked-out surprised.

"I was in the neighborhood," I tell him, which, naturally, since I'm here, is the truth.

"Come on in." He's got on jeans and Keds and a T-shirt. And looks younger and shorter. He looks like a kid who ought to have a baseball glove hanging on his bedroom wall, and some old posters, and a pile of dirty clothes that his mom in an apron is hollering at him to pick up before supper.

He takes me into the house, which is one of those where you walk right into the living room. (The kind Glenna turns up her nose at because it doesn't have an entry hall that lets you put up a mirror and a nice little table.) It has tan carpet and tan wallpaper, and windows that are so covered up with filmy tan curtains and tan liners and tan valances that you can't be sure there are really windows there. Maybe the Dawsons have blank walls that they've fixed up to look like windows. People who have nothing to hide, Mom always says, don't give a second thought to closing up everything tight as a drum as they don't have to worry about looking suspicious. So they don't; they look like they can't stand the sight of who is moving in next door. My guess would be that the back windows of the house are nailed shut, just to be on the safe side. Because you never know these days who might come around, even to your house on Rosewood.

His dad and mom are busy. That's another thing I learned from Mom. When kids come over for lessons, or whenever someone rings the doorbell that you're not expecting, you have to have your busy business already set up, ready to go. Because people think it's strange if you're just sitting there, or (worse) lying there, and aren't busy. Especially in subdivisions. (Although I imagine it applies even more to changing neighborhoods like this one. People who aren't busy around here are more than likely up to trouble.)

L.W.'s mom is ironing. She looks about as happy as some film star who is climbing into bed with her lover at the end of a big slash and splatter scene. She looks happy as a pig. I get a fleeting thought that if Mom had thought of ironing first, she might never have had to mess with piano teaching. But I guess ironing—if you charge money for it—isn't an acceptable thing in the subdivisions. You couldn't put out a sign IRONING DONE HERE in this neighborhood, even in the window, tucked in front of a tan shade. But here is Mrs. L.W. Senior looking as if she's on some kind of heavenly fix, steam-ironing gores cut on the bias, gussets set into dolmans, jabots tacked onto plackets, zapping each garment with a jet of spray starch before bearing down with the hot iron.

And not the least bit embarrassed to be ironing right in the living room, with the TV set not even turned on for an excuse. (That opens another idea to me—that maybe people who pretend to get the ironing done while they're watching the soaps are really getting the soaps done as a cover for doing the ironing. That maybe there are a lot of clean activities we're ashamed to admit we like to do.)

The house is the vintage that has a dining room through an archway, one almost as big as the living room. There, L.W.'s dad, who is fat where Mrs. L.W. is skinny, is working away at the big table, working real hard over something, a bunch of papers. But he gets to his feet when I come in, to be properly introduced.

"Dad, this is my friend from acting class, Jolene Temple. She was in the neighborhood."

It turns out his dad is a fanatic about something called the Perpetual Fixed Monthly Calendar. He tells me—and L.W. stands around trying to indicate that he has probably heard all this one million times—that names more famous than his have supported the PFMC: the presidents of General Motors and General Electric, the inventor of the camera and the Model T. He shows me a great green chart on the wall. "With thirteen months of twenty-eight days each," he says, "every week and every month begins on Sunday. To know the date is to know the day: if it's the second, it has to be Monday; all Saturdays are multiples of seven. We have to put to rest the wandering week. You get the idea, little lady?"

"Yes sir," I say, amazed. Because of how simple it seems, and how easy that would be to use. I don't stop to multiply thirteen times twenty-eight (sure they've done that and it comes out right), but wonder how we ever got mixed up with the system we have. That also gives me a feeling of awe, L.W. Senior does, at a man his age and size finding something so orderly to be interested in, so logical to be pursuing. I think how frustrated he must feel, this old man (who looks, both the Dawsons do, old enough to be my grandparents, as old as Hoyt and Cissy), that everybody doesn't see the wisdom and want to adopt his calendar. He must feel that the rest of the world has decided to fall into chaos when there isn't any need to.

L.W. asks me if I'd like to go get something to eat, and I say sure. I get the idea that we aren't going to visit here in this wonderful, busy house. That he is a little embarrassed by his folks, and doesn't know that I think they're just about perfect.

I imagine the two of them getting up in the morning and beginning with their work—her sprinkling the ironing and him calculating dates—and them doing that all day long except when they stop to eat, in the kitchen so as not to bother Lenox Worth's papers in the dining room. And then maybe allowing themselves just one more round before bedtime.

I smile at both the Dawsons and wait for L.W. by the tan divan.

He says, "Mom, we're going to get something to eat," as if she hasn't heard him already say that.

"Be careful, Buddy," she says, showing some very white false teeth. "Nice to meet you, Jolene."

"Yes, indeed," his dad calls after us as we exit the house through the lassoed door.

15

"*L*IFE FOLLOWS ART," L.W. says, when we actually do find a diner out San Pedro, complete with even the sign in the window, a slick white printed plastic sign that says: EAT HERE OR WE'LL BOTH STARVE.

We sit in the back at the last of a narrow row of booths. Nobody else is there except at the front counter a couple of women—who look as if they work nearby, probably at one of the big franchises—are having coffee and a semi-private talk.

"What'll it be, folks?"

"Do you have grits?" L.W. asks, giving me a sweet glance.

"Hash browns," the big man in the apron says.

"Has to be grits."

"You want grits we got grits." He wanders to the front and reaches up over the grill, behind the individual Corn Flakes and Sugar Pops boxes, brushing away the swirl of dust around his head. He pulls out a little box of instant white cornmeal, opens it, pours hot water from a glass pot used for tea, and, with his other hand, refills the cups of the women at the counter. "What else, ladies," he says.

It's awkward, being with L.W. in the diner.

The two times we were together before, we were both acting. That was okay. We could do our parts. But here, now, in the booth, we're supposed not to be acting any more. Here is the real us—and that's the problem. I guess who we're being is Buddy and the Niece, which is as close as we can probably get to being ourselves.

I've dressed, now that I think about it, as a niece, in a flowered skirt, long cotton sweater in bright green, orange socks, and Reeboks.

"What were you doing in the neighborhood?" L.W. asks, as nervous as I am.

Naturally, I can't tell him that in my panic over Mom's card and Dad's letter to Brogan, I thought maybe I could come live with him. Somebody who I only met two times in public places. Somebody whose folks are always home, ironing flounces and calculating Wednesdays.

"I wanted to see you," I tell him. "I liked meeting you and then we didn't run into each other any more."

"That was something, switching parts."

"Are you really an actor?" I look at L.W. with a lot of interest, at his good worn-out jeans and his good really used T-shirt. His Buddy sort of face that is very close to mine at the moment.

He explains that he's a drama student at Trinity, graduate level. Then says proudly, "I'm writing a play."

"No kidding?"

"It's not my first," he says. "I had another, back in high school, that got a prize in a one-act contest. It was called *Under Brown Umbrella*."

I repeat the name, *Under Brown Umbrella*, because I can tell he is half in love with the words. Naturally, I assume it's about the oil bust and that brown means crude oil. I give him a big smile, pleased with myself for figuring it out.

L.W. takes time out to thank the man for our bowls of lukewarm grits and to find out that his name is not Pete but Al—but that's okay, the idea is the same. The diner seems like a high school set, with its plastic sign, its instant cornmeal, and Al himself, who is trying to do his big-bellied best, but who keeps forgetting and looking at the clock, wishing the scene was over and done for the day and him home with a long-neck Lone Star.

"I'm getting more through-action in the new play." L.W. brings us back to his subject. *"The Second Peloponnesian War."*

Again, I repeat the name, so he can enjoy hearing it. Although this time I can't figure out the point—but then my history isn't very good. "What's it about?" I ask, not wanting to show my ignorance and hoping I'm not supposed to figure out some obvious classical connection.

"They're both about the big thing that's happening today in Texas: bilingual education. One of those issues that the state is always getting mixed up on. The liberals—who ought to be the ones saying that we should all speak a common language if we're going to be equal—are the ones fighting *for* it. And the conservatives—who you'd think would be the ones arguing that a separate language will keep the Mexicans in their place—are the ones *against* it. They've got it backwards." He looks to see if I'm following his reasoning. "So I got the idea of showing that on the stage. Of showing, I mean, that each side is supporting its own worst case."

Bilingual education? I am totally surprised. *I* thought that what was happening in Texas right this minute was Aunt Glenna Rose and her MasterCards, and Uncle Brogan worrying about Chapter Eleven. I can't think of anything to say to L.W.

Bilingual education, I want to tell him, is one of those things like unisex bathrooms that politicians and the press talk about all the time but nobody listens to. Because if you need to pee all you want is some place right then and there, and it doesn't matter what it says on the door (EMPLOYEES ONLY, DAMES, GENTS). The same if you're trying to find your way to the gate in the airport or across the border. It doesn't matter what the sign says or which language it says it in;

somebody points the way to you. Nobody in public places has much of a language anyway—they just grunt and point and scratch their heads. You know if you were playing the part of somebody in a public transportation place or voting place or eating place, you'd have maybe six lines in the whole script.

"I don't know if you've noticed it"—L.W. leans over—"but most people quit listening the very minute you say anything about educational issues."

"Is that right?"

"That's what you can do with a play, get past that resistance. I mean, you can reach the audience in a way that you never could if you were running around carrying a signboard that said BILINGUAL EDUCATION IS UNILATERAL DISARMAMENT."

"You're right about that."

"California has already passed a law declaring English the state language, and you'll see, Jolene. One of these days there'll be a governor out there or a senator whose family came from Mexico. And he'll be in office because he speaks English." Here L.W. realizes what he's said and looks at me, embarrassed. "Or *she*."

But that doesn't bother me. I'm not sitting in the booth at this plastic imitation of Pete's diner (which is really Al's) worrying whether I'm getting insulted by L.W.'s not thinking that the state of California is going to elect a woman governor one day. Or a Mexican either. Or another old Hollywood actor with a wrinkled neck.

"Actually," he says, changing the topic slightly, "it's a collaboration, the new one. This other actor and I, Archie Leach, are doing it together. The actual writing."

"I've heard that name."

He laughs. "Everybody is going to think that. It's a great stage name. It's Cary Grant's real name. When he died it was in all the magazines and papers, so everybody has heard it and seen it, but they won't remember where."

"The way everybody knows who Norma Jean was?"

"The exact same thing. Somebody would have been smart about ten years ago to use that name. Somebody wanting to get into films."

I have a minute, just a minute, of wishing that he wasn't working on his play with someone else, but that doesn't last long. I guess my real fear is that if somebody is with him all the time, then what with the ironing board and perpetual weeks, that doesn't leave much of L.W. for me.

"I'd like to see the play when you finish," I tell him.

"Maybe you'll come when we put it on."

"Maybe."

He hesitates. "I really was surprised to see you standing on the porch at home."

"I couldn't get up my nerve to phone. I was afraid you wouldn't remember my name."

"Sure I did. But Jolene Temple wasn't listed in the phone book."

"I live with my aunt and uncle."

"Where are your parents?"

"They're separated, and both of them move around a lot in their jobs, so, you know, it was more stable to live with my uncle and his wife. I moved here in ninth grade. I guess one of these days I ought to be looking for a place of my own. It's hard to make yourself leave, when you've got a room and all."

"The same with me. I'm twenty-five. That's too old to be living at home. But I took a year off to work, year and a half, really, to get the tuition. Trinity costs an arm and leg. So it made sense to stay home, save money. Mom and Dad don't want me moving anyway. They wouldn't have anybody to talk to but each other. Both of them there all day—my dad's retired, he's on a pension; my mom took early retirement—they don't have a lot to say to each other." He looks as if he thinks he's confiding something personal. As if having parents content to be in the same room all day every day with each other was something to be ashamed about.

"What I was really doing in the neighborhood"—I look at him and then look away, having just come up with a great idea—"was coming to see if you'd like to go to a party with me."

"Sure I would."

"My uncle and aunt are giving a party for his clients, he sells car phones, at the La Fonda Sur Rosa in a couple of weeks."

"The Sub Rosa."

"That's right. I was thinking, you and I have been to two parties together already, in a way." This is where the hard part comes in, so I slow down. I wait a minute, wanting him to get the drift of what I'm asking.

"That was a coincidence, wasn't it?"

"I thought, since you did the broker at Zona Rosa—"

He gets the idea right away, and looks like he doesn't mind at all, which makes me weak in the knees, or would, if I were standing up. Because it means he's going to think it's okay to be acting a part at my folks' party.

"You want me to do that again?" he asks.

"That'd be just swell. Just swell. I could tell them that I've been dating this investment banker."

That reminds him of something, I can tell by his face. "You still seeing that painter?"

I hold my head up to show I'm not embarrassed. "I pose for him regularly. He pays a lot. I'm saving up so I can move out."

"What's his name?"

"Henry Wozencrantz."

"You're kidding."

"Why would I be kidding?"

"Around here that's like saying his name is Van Gogh. I mean, he's the most famous painter in San Antonio. In the Southwest. He's like Whistler or something. You know what I mean. I mean he's really famous. He gets written up every time he has a show. Or they'll do a feature on something like Southwest Art, I'm talking about *Life* or *Time,* and there'll be the usual stuff with big Indians and red mountains, and then there'll be Wozencrantz, with his brown-toned paintings that look like daguerreotypes."

Henry, famous? The boy whose uncle had a mistress with a china hand? I try to think if that can be so. I remember that he acted like I should recognize his name at the Sun Dog, but then that was a gathering of artists and he was an artist.

For a minute I get an uneasy feeling, but then it goes away. For one thing, what L.W. says doesn't sound like the slides that Henry showed me, the beautiful shapes that turned out to be shoulders and knees. For another, I figure L.W. is just repeating what he's heard, dropping in at openings, picking up the language for later use.

"What about you, if I'm the broker?" L.W. gets back to the topic of the party.

"I told Aunt Glenna I was working as a model. She took that to mean fashion. Me, a fashion model?" I make it a sort of joke, to see if he thinks I can get away with that.

"You'd be great." He sounds like he means it. "The new trend. Calvin Klein. Perry Ellis." He looks me over. "You've got the cool look."

"You think so?"

"Sure," he says. "It's not much of a variation on your poet."

And I say, like I was picking up on a cue, "These are the best grits west of Natchez," and we smile, safe into our parts again.

16

"ACCORDING TO HOYT, they lost their hotels on Baltic and Mediterranean last night." Over breakfast, Brogan is giving Glenna an update on his folks.

I'm there between them, the interested third party they like, finishing my buttered toast.

"Oh, shit." Glenna has her hair rolled up and is in an old pair of Brogan's pajamas that she likes to wear to sit around and have juice when they're not doing business. "Oh, damn. How can they do it again? You tell me. Don't they know there's nobody to bail them out any more?"

"Hoyt was cased on coverall."

"Don't speak to me in that foreign language."

"Cissy was cased on B 17."

"Bingo. They were playing bingo."

"You got it."

"How in this wide world is it possible to lose the mortgage on your house in a *bingo game?*"

"Easy. That's when they always do it. It's never craps. It's never blackjack. Those are too rich for their blood."

"I don't understand."

"Blackjack you got to have money to stay in the game. Craps you got sharks watching every move. Bingo, down there in the bingo parlors, you got a running total and you got all these old folks playing with their social security, looking like they're at a church social, and first thing you know you're down five hundred, and there goes the house payment. And then if you're already two months behind, the bank can decide that it especially wants, right now in the squeeze, to own that little frame doodad with the sweet gum in the backyard.

Bankers start sitting around getting nostalgic to own Lot 4, Block 48 one more time. Like in the good old days."

"Why wouldn't the bank just look the other way? They got houses out the kazoo they can't sell right this minute."

"Repossessed house goes in Column B. Moves from Column A. Moves from accounts receivable to assets. Looks good on paper. They got nothing but accounts receivable, they got nothing but uncollected debts, an examiner could say. See here, they can tell him, we got this two bedroom, eat-in kitchen, all the extras, Lot 4, Block 48. We're fixing to have a couple more. This is your solvent bank, with assets."

"They couldn't sell it for twenty-five thousand, that place."

"Multiply by three. Times three. You could sell a leaking dog house for seventy-five G in that part of town."

"Did you forget the bottom fell out?"

"So lien-fettered upward mobes have got to drop their one ninety-nines and move down in a hurry. But they got to keep their kids in the Alamo Heights even if they're eating Alpo. So here comes this little bungalow on the right side of all the tracks. No way it won't be a hot item."

"If we bought it, could we make a profit selling it?" She takes a finger and smooths the wrinkle between her eyes.

"I'm not putting Hoyt and Cissy on the street. Besides, in three years we can get double. There's going to be a turnaround, you'll see."

"Brogan, paying for this customers' party is already breaking the piggy bank."

"I'm coming up with something."

"I saw the flyers of your cocoa king." She sniffs.

"Something new. I got an idea. Give me a little time to polish the fine points. The bank's giving Hoyt and Cissy thirty days' notice. To come up with the back payments, P-I-T-I, principal, interest, taxes, insurance."

"This is eight times since I've known you, Brogan Temple,

they've done this. Seven times we bought the house back, starting on our honeymoon. We got a box big enough for a Kelvinator holding deeds to that place."

"You got to understand the urge." Brogan is full of sympathy for his parents. "It's excitement. What're you going to do at seventy years with no dough and nothing to do but watch the tube and you can't see too well for that? And you've given up smoking because your doctor doesn't understand it's your only occupation; so you're retired from the only thing you ever knew how to do well.

"And you fight a little, but they never got a lot of pleasure from that, and you shop some, but that takes money. Besides, you don't know what to buy that you don't already have too many of. Their house looks like a three-car garage sale already. But you can get in the Pontiac and drive across town and then you get in the atmosphere of winning. You get *that close*." He holds up his fingers half an inch apart. "You get that close to the big one. Maybe even win fifty or a hundred. That feels great. It makes you forget you lost three."

"Your mom never gambled, did she?" Glenna turns to me for some third-party sympathy.

I consider how to answer this. Gambling, you could say, is all Mom ever did. But not that way, no, not bingo. "No," I tell her.

"Brogan doesn't gamble."

I don't see how she can sit here and say that, but she's thinking about being cased for coverall. About waiting there with your favorite bingo card lacking only that one number and you're going to win one thousand dollars when they call it. Brogan doesn't do *that*.

"You worry sometimes it's inherited," she says. "Like heavy drinking, or being color-blind." She looks at me. "I bet if I had kids, I'd be a nervous wreck, worrying were they placing bets on Little League or something."

"The first time," Brogan says in a solemn voice, helping himself to a sweet roll, "the first time it happened, Hoyt called me up and said, 'Son, we lost our hotels on Boardwalk and Park Place.' This time he said, 'On Baltic and Mediterranean.' It's real sad, isn't it, hon, how when the bottom falls out your image of yourself deteriorates."

17

$\mathcal{M}$OM ALWAYS had a soft spot for that house on Savoy Street, her parents' lime green asbestos-siding house with its gravel roof and its turning-brown elephant ears in the run-down neighborhood with the high-class names: Jade, Plaza, Empire, Astoria.

If she'd had the money and we hadn't been on the run, it would have been her and not Brogan who bought back Lot 4, Block 48 every time Hoyt and Cissy lost it to the bank.

We lived in the house in the early years of my life, but I don't remember the time when things were good between Mom and Dad. My first clear memories are of what she calls the Running Hot and Cold Phase, between the purchase of the World Books and the Tour de France tickets in the Christmas stocking.

Their scenes in those days went something like this. Dad would stand there—feeling his bare crown and rocking back and forth on his heels—shouting that if Mom wanted to go off on some wild goose chase that was her prerogative and no business of his, but that he wasn't having any child of his chasing geese, no thank you, ma'am, and that if Mom wasn't interested in his normal life, he'd be glad to give it to someone else, namely his daughter; then Mom would counter that if Dad wanted to miss out on seeing the sights and having the adventures of this one-time lifetime that was his private problem, but that she had no intention of depriving certain people—for instance, her daughter—of a ringside seat on Experience.

Then Dad would storm out to a motel until it was time to hit the road for a week of selling his drilling-rig supplies, and they'd both have a chance to cool down.

Mom was still a little bit in love with Dad, I think, in those days. For one thing, he reminded her of Uncle Brogan. Both of them, hefty men, had this problem with their hair: they were losing it. When I was really little, Dad and my uncle were combing long slicked-down strands over their bald spots. Later, when Dad was grabbing me off playgrounds and out of churches, he and Brogan both had moved to fat dark wavy hairpieces that sat on their heads like caps. (I guess that by now Dad has followed Brogan's lead again and is having them weave a kind of bird's nest on his head with his own and borrowed hair.)

So Mom would stew for a few days, say that we were going to move on, that it wasn't working out staying in the same city with this man whom she'd married too young, that he was nothing but a crimp in her style. Then she'd weaken and start to think about a *reconciliation*, as she called it.

Then, when it was time for Dad to wheel back into town, if she was in the mood to indicate that the coast was clear, that Dad could come in, cozy up on the couch, watch me turn the pages of the World Books, bring in his sample bags and stay the night, she'd send him their signal: one of Hoyt's white handkerchiefs tied outside on the porch rail.

This game made constant arguments between her and Cissy.

"You are giving up, is what that says," Cissy claimed. "A white flag means surrender."

"A white flag is a temporary truce," Mom insisted. "It means stop shooting. Red Cross waves a white flag on the battlefield. Generals on horseback who're getting together to talk things over wave white flags. It means Don't shoot."

"I say it's plain as day surrender."

"It's a cease-fire is what it is."

Theirs was typical of all the arguments in our family, because the matter wasn't anything that either of them, Mom or Cissy, was about to settle by looking it up or calling a library. They just liked to have a topic to debate, to exercise their minds and show that there were two sides to every question.

As it turned out, the white handkerchief made fights between Mom and Dad, too.

I remember a typical time.

It was one sunny winter afternoon right after a bitter cold norther. Seeing from what was flapping in the strong wind that hostilities were suspended for the moment, Dad pulled up out front in one of the big rattling showy clunkers that he liked to drive in those days, came up the steps and marched in the front door.

"I get the distinct impression you're leaning toward a reconciliation," he said to Mom. "Glad to know it. In my opinion it's time for things to warm up."

"Where'd you get that big idea?" Mom asked him, shooing me over in a corner, patting the sofa beside her.

"That white thing you put out there. Means you give up, is how I read it. A white flag means a person gives up. Correct me if I'm wrong."

"Wrong, wrong, wrong," Mom said.

Then they picked up where they left off on the old fight, until finally Dad stalked out of the house on Savoy—with its falling-down porch, its one-car garage, its sagging palmetto.

"The cease-fire has ceased," Mom hollered at his back, as she crammed Hoyt's white hanky in the trash.

18

"WE'RE GOING to a show," Henry says after he's wrapped me in the sheet and put the flowers back in their vase.

I know he doesn't mean a film; show to Henry means art. "Is it an opening?" I'm excited by the idea. I haven't been out anywhere with Henry since we went to see the cow skulls and to meet his mother. "Who shall I be?" Last time I wore the banker's suit because I was being an antique dealer; but he may have another idea this time.

"Indian," he says. "It's an exhibit of Navajo blankets, on loan from Dallas."

"Little d," I say, using Brogan's name for the rival city.

"Little show, more than likely, but I want to see it."

When I have my skirt on, which is deep blue and comes almost to my ankles, and a white shirt I wear a lot because it's really loose and has no collar, he walks behind me and braids some blue yarn into my hair. He puts a silver belt on me and the turquoise necklace, and then he rubs some dark color across my forehead and nose and chin and cheeks.

I look in the antler mirror when he's done, and it's amazing. I could be weaving on a loom at the show and nobody would give me a second glance.

. . .

The blankets, it turns out, aren't in a gallery like the Sun Dog, but at a little museum called the Bernais which is really a very old mansion where you step down onto a cool tile floor and where there are lots of carvings around the ceiling. Right inside the door is a table with flyers about a Game Show Auction that's coming up in the fall, and glossy catalogues about today's collection.

Henry gets permission to take some pictures, even though there are about a half-dozen signs that say NO PHOTOGRAPHS MAY BE TAKEN OF THIS EXHIBIT, because the curator is bobbing around all excited that a real artist is here.

While the jumpy man talks to Henry and Henry is snapping away, I read about the hangings. The brochure says that the ancestors of the Navajos came up out of the bowels of the earth to this world. That they lived in a sacred place surrounded by four mountains (four is their magic number) and that their baby girls were propped up in their cradles so that they could watch their mothers weave. That each baby's hands were rubbed with spider webs, so that she would grow up weaving, too.

Henry wants me to come with him. He is looking at everything very fast, which is his way. Finally, he stops at two beautiful blankets, both striped, thin stripes, in white, brown, blue, and red. He feels the blankets although there are signs that say DO NOT TOUCH, but again the curator—who is talking to him nonstop the whole time—doesn't mind at all. He even helps Henry lift the bottom of one serape-style to feel the weight of it.

The red, the man explains, is raveled Spanish flannel in this one, but over here the red is cochineal, which is made from crushed insects.

Henry isn't listening. He has me stand in front of one of the striped ones and then another. Then he moves me to one with red triangles and fatter stripes.

The man tells him that the pattern in that one goes all the way back to the Arab invasion of Spain in the seven hundreds, maybe to China before that. And would Henry like to see the documentation?

"Here," Henry says to me, "stand here and face it. Turn your back."

So I do. I turn my back and stand real close to the blanket until I am almost touching it and I put my hands on it, too, since that seems to be all right. I get into my part, imagining that I'm learning to weave from the way the red yarn and carded indigo wool thread themselves into diamonds and stripes. That the pattern is magically in my hands, and that my hands can make this pattern that no other baby girl will ever grow up knowing how to make.

Then I hear a voice say, "Jolene, is it?" and I freeze. What if it's Henry's mother? (Of course it is, because I recognize that skimpy straight-up-and-down gray voice.) She will see me being an Indian instead of an antique dealer. I have a moment of total panic, but then I remember that Henry is here, and calm down. He will know what to do.

"Hello, Mother," he says, not sounding surprised that she has appeared.

The curator bustles around even faster now, like he's decided that something really important is going on in his cool old museum.

I turn around, looking at Henry.

"You remember my mother," he says casually to me. To her he says, "My good fortune to have found myself a most satisfactory model."

"Hello, Mrs. Wozencrantz." I hold out my hand, which naturally doesn't know the first thing about weaving any more, because the spell is broken.

She barely looks at me but says to Henry, "Do come say hello, won't you, just for a moment." She gestures to two ladies a few feet away who look just like her. "You remember Millie, from the Friends of the Bernais, and Hallie, from the Friends of the Fine Arts? Just say hello, won't you? It gives them such a thrill to say they've seen you."

"I'm working."

"One minute, please."

"Come on," he says to me.

He kisses the cheeks of the two women in gray who are so thin you could blow them over like paper dolls in their floating dresses.

"Is that Karen?" one of them whispers, noticing me.

"Hush," the other whispers back.

"This is Henry's model," Mrs. Wozencrantz says smoothly, as if my being that was old news to her and she'd known it all along. "Models are back in fashion," she tells her friends. "Since, well, really before all that to-do about Wyeth. He was simply part of the trend. No doubt he'd been holding them for years, until it was the fashion again. Soon we'll be back to figure studies entirely, isn't that so, Henry?"

"Back to the seventeenth century like everything else," the one called Millie pronounces.

"The more things change—" the one named Hallie murmurs, then speaks in French (real French, not like Glenna's).

"Won't you two join us for a bite of lunch at Lou Tess?" Mrs. Wozencrantz asks Henry. "We'd so like that."

"I'm working," Henry tells her, and hurries me off down a long wall of striped blankets to a new one that he likes, a yellow and orange and black and white chief-style blanket. He has me do it again, turn my face to the wall and stand there against the red bands made by the raveled Spanish flannel.

Then he doesn't take pictures any more, or even seem to remember I'm there. When I get tired and turn around, hoping the dark smudges on my face haven't wiped off on the stripes, he doesn't even notice.

After a while I sit cross-legged on the floor and go back to reading about the Navajos while the ladies back down the hall talk and talk to the curator, and Henry paints and paints in his head.

19

$\mathcal{T}$HE NEXT DAY the phone rings at Glenna's, and when I answer it (not thinking) a familiar voice floats in my ear.

"Think of a number between one and three."

"Two," I say numbly to the dial tone.

Two what?

Two when?

20

$\mathcal{A}$S I PARK in front of L.W.'s house on Rosewood, I notice that there's one of those trees with green bark in the yard. I guess I didn't see it last time. Glenna and Cissy are always arguing about those trees. Cissy saying that they're called huisache; Glenna that no sir they're retamas.

Their argument is a lot like Mom and Cissy's about the white flag (does it mean truce or surrender?): it isn't going anywhere. That is, neither one of them is ever going to check in some tree book and see for sure which tree has leaves like needles and a green bark. Because in my family nobody really wants to risk being the loser in a fight.

I'm convinced that's why Mom and Dad finally let me move in with Glenna and Brogan, because otherwise with all the stealing back and forth, one day one of them was going to get backed into a corner and have to get a lawyer and have a court case. And then some judge would get to settle once and for all who I really belonged to.

This way, I can see that I'll be sixty years old and Mom will still be claiming, She's mine because I raised her, and Dad will still be insisting, She's mine because I gave her a normal life, and Brogan and Glenna will be swearing, She's ours because we provided her a decent home and a college education.

I'm thinking about all that when I park my car and look at the green-barked tree, whatever it is, because I'm wishing I could disappear for good into L.W.'s house. Become a fixture like his mom in the living room ironing on her puffed sleeves and his dad at the dining table putting to rest the wandering week. Jolene in the kitchen, say, making chocolate chip cookies with toasted pecans and condensed milk, pulling the hot trays out of the oven, having reversed them top to bottom and front to back twice during the baking to be sure they are all even, calling to the rest of the household, "Come and get it, you all." Pouring four glasses of cold milk to set on the counter.

I see it like the opening of a play. The curtain goes up and Mom spits on the iron to see if it's hot enough and Pop wets the tip of his pencil and shuffles some papers—they're on either side of the stage—then, upstage, Buddy is sitting on his single bed under a hanging light bulb smacking his fist into a baseball glove, while downstage the Niece is pulling the trays out of the oven with two big potholders shaped like puppies.

Mom's call has put the fear in me for sure.

21

I WAS SURPRISED when L.W. asked me over out of the blue, and I'm even more surprised when I get inside. Something looks strange, and it takes me a minute to grasp the fact that his folks aren't home.

At least his mom isn't busy inside the front door and his dad isn't through the arch bending over charts. In fact, the ironing board is put up, and the dining table is set for dinner with a thick lace cloth and big white napkins tucked through wooden rings.

"Where's everybody?"

L.W. looks embarrassed. "They go shopping on Saturdays. That's why I invited you over. They always did that when they both worked, did all the grocery shopping and got the car washed and picked up the cleaning, all that. They got in the habit. I think to go out now in the middle of the week would be to admit they're idle, and they won't do that. So Saturday is still shopping day. Then Sunday they go to Church of Christ." He hesitates. "But they aren't gone as long on Sunday."

I try to put him at his ease. "It was a good time for me to get away. My aunt and uncle are pretty frantic about this party they're having next week."

He nods. "Want a Coke?"

"Okay." I don't really like carbonated drinks, but I'm being friendly.

When we get our Diet Coke cans, he leads me down the hall, past the bathroom, to his bedroom. He's jumpy as a cat about taking me in there, because I guess it shows what's on his mind, and why it matters how long his folks are going to be gone. But I'm really glad, because of what he's thinking and to get to see his room, which I've imagined a lot.

Sure enough, there's a baseball glove on the wall, and also about a dozen jackets and sweaters and caps, even cowboy hats, all hanging on hooks over the end of his bed. The bed is pushed against the wall, so that the stuff on hooks makes a sort of headboard.

He sits on the bed, still nervous, and I sit right down beside him. But then, instead of what I'm naturally expecting, he starts to talk about—bilingual education.

"You don't see other immigrants around here, Czechs, Germans, Swedes, insisting that their kids get educated and their old people get to vote in their native language. They get over here and the first thing, they take English as a second language, and they pass the test and then they have English as a first language. And their children win the Westinghouse Science Fair and they don't walk around all the time with a signboard on advertising the fact they're foreign."

"You're right about that."

"Well, in *The Second Peloponnesian War*—"

And then I see that he's been leading up to his play again, and repeat the title so he can admire it.

"—I've got a Czech and a German, played by Archie and me, and they argue about what language the main character should speak. He's the Mexican. They argue over him like two dogs over a bone. He's the bone. And all the time all he wants is to speak the cash language."

"That would make a good title, *Cash Language*." I'm trying to be agreeable.

But suddenly L.W. looks at his watch. His face turns red and he places a hand on my knee. "Here I am letting the time get away from us, Jolene. And they'll be coming back before long."

Then I relax, because I know now he really wants to do it after all. Here on this neat bed under the hooks with all the hats and sweaters. I like that. Quick as a wink I pull off my blouse and kick off my shoes. I pull up my skirt and then look at his face and stop. He's just staring at me.

I take off my panties, but his nervousness is catching. If he thinks we're going to have trouble, then maybe we are.

"What do you like?" I ask him, real friendly, trying to get things going.

"I don't want to just get you in the house and then lunge at you," he says, leaning over to give me a deep kiss. "But not having a place of my own yet, when they're gone—"

"I like you a lot." I help him with his belt.

"You sure?"

"Let's do it, and then we can go to the diner before they get back."

"Is that okay?"

I kiss him some more and then help him out of his jeans. What I see I like a lot; he's got a wonderful build and I'm ready for him as soon as I see what he's got.

The bed is narrow, so he helps me up on top, and I close my eyes and ride until he comes. I mean he comes almost as soon as I start, so then I don't know what to do. Because I thought I'd come first a couple of times and then we'd rock awhile and then do whatever he wanted.

He wraps his arms around me and holds me real tight, saying my name over and over, in a sort of singsong way, Jo-leen, Jo-leen, and it's the first time I've really liked my name.

Then he isn't moving any more, and I don't know what I'm supposed to do. Get off?

But the problem is solved in an awful way, because at that

moment we hear the front door open, and someone—his mom—calls out, "Buddy?"

I grab my clothes and he grabs his and we're dressed in two seconds flat while we hear the sound of sacks being dumped on the floor and the door being closed.

L.W. looks at me and I look at him. I'm not worrying about them as much as he is, because I'm still sort of confused and wishing I'd had time to come.

We hear a woman's heels clicking down the hall floor toward L.W.'s room.

Then the back door opens and a girl's voice calls, "Anybody home?"

"Archie," he whispers.

Before they get to us, he pulls a sweater off a hook and throws it around my shoulders. Then, instead of moving farther away or standing up, he scoots over until he's sitting right up against me with his arm around me. He grabs a Diet Coke can and is feeding me sips from it when his mom and a wide-faced girl in a jumper meet at his doorway.

"Hi, Mrs. Dawson," the girl says.

"Hello, Archie."

"Buddy?" His mom stops dead when she sees me.

"Something wrong?" Archie stops, too.

"It's okay," L.W. says in a real serious voice. "It's okay. She's okay. Aren't you, Jolene?"

"I guess so." I haven't yet got the drift of the scene we're playing, so I sort of lower my head and swallow.

"She had a terrible scare," he explains. "Mugged—"

They look at him and he tightens his arm around me.

"—at the diner on San Pedro. How she had the presence of mind to drive here—"

"I didn't know where else—" I wipe one eye with the back of my hand.

"Gracious!" Mrs. Dawson sucks in her breath.

"Gee, are you hurt?" The girl bounds into the room.

"You were really brave," L.W. prompts me.

I take a breath and plunge into it. "I guess I got so mad at him that I didn't have sense enough to be scared. I just hit him for all I was worth. I hope he's not still lying in the street. The fat guy—"

"Al, at the diner."

"—stuck his head out when he saw there was trouble. I guess he called the police."

The girl makes a face. "And they haven't showed up yet, I bet."

"Arch, this is Jolene Temple. Remember, I told you?"

"Sure, the poet."

"Arch and I—" He turns to me.

I look up and smile bravely, overcoming my recent fright. "Why, you're the one working on the play."

"That's right." She sits down on the bed, too.

"I'll just make us all some tea." Mrs. Dawson hurries off to intercept Mr. Dawson in the hall and whisper that that girl in there was *attacked* right out in broad daylight. And we hear him boom that no place is safe any more, that you can't set foot outside your door, that they're *everywhere*.

I hadn't got the idea from L.W. before that the student clever enough to take Cary Grant's real name was a girl. Right away I have to wonder if she knows what we've been up to. To wonder if she's ridden L.W. herself, out of his jeans right here on this little bed. I have to wonder if she can smell the sex.

Surely she can. I look over at her, expecting her to be furious. But she seems at home in the way that a friend would be, some guy that had been tossing baseballs with L.W. since maybe third grade. Pal. That's what she looks like, a pal.

The idea comes to me that maybe while we're being Buddy and the Niece and she's being the Pal, that what she'd really like would be to be undressed and all over L.W. like a case of the measles for about twenty-four hours. But I could be wrong. I could be projecting. If I'd come to see L.W. and knew where the back door was, and that I was welcome to come right in without knocking, I'd sure know he'd been screwing the girl with the mussed-up hair and mashed around just-kissed face whose panties were still shoved up under the pillow at the head of the little bed.

But Pal doesn't seem bothered one bit. She jumps up and goes off to help his mom get the tea, giving us a minute alone.

L.W. looks wrung out.

"No sweat," I whisper, grabbing my red cotton briefs and stuffing them in my bag. "You did great. That was some improvising." I give him a slow kiss before I get out of there. "See you at the Sub Rosa."

Then I'm down the hall and out the door.

Standing by the retama/huisache, I let out my breath. One thing has been definitely decided: L.W.'s house is no place to disappear into.

22

*O*N PASS-OF-THE-CAMELS PARK I was a movie star.

That's the subdivision we moved to after the Terminix "man" stole me out of the hall at school. The Suburb of Suburbs Mom called it, and it was. Acres of homes, miles of homes, a maze of homes. It had three basic models which repeated eenie, meenie, miney, and then repeated in mirror image, miney, meenie, eenie again. There was the basic one-story ranch, the split-level ranch, and the two-story saltbox. We had a ranch split reverse, in which the piano pupils had to step down into the living room that Mom christened the Practice Hall.

To understand something about the child star routine, you first have to understand something about El Paso where our 'burb was located. For starts, it's the westernmost part of the state, although it isn't what's commonly called West Texas, being too high and too dry. Picture a desert in the mountains. For another, it's on the time zone of Phoenix and Tucson instead of little d and San Antone.

(You can get the idea if you think about the fact that our move from Texarkana to El Paso is the same distance as from El Paso to L.A. or Texarkana to Savannah; the same as from New York City to Florida or San Francisco to Canada, for those people who get all the states in the middle mixed up. Or from London, England to Florence, Italy, for the international set.)

But that's geography, which is only another way to say that day to day and person to person we were in another world out there in Pass-of-the-Camels Park from where we'd been in Honey Grove Hills in East Texas.

Mom, making a dry run around the playground of the elementary school our bunch of houses fed into, decided— seeing that everybody was tanned dark as an Indian and that everybody's hair was dry as a tumbleweed and that they all wore boots and jeans, boys and girls—that I was going to stand out like a sore thumb and she'd better turn that to my advantage.

She studied the terrain and came to the conclusion that it was a safe bet that people who lived in what was really the western part of the U.S., instead of the Texas part of it, were going to be taking their cues from Hollywood. So that was the basis of her plan.

I entered school a month late, with a pale face, dark curly

hair, short ruffled skirt, and sunglasses. I mean if you see a kid in third grade with shades on you think either that she's blind and wonder where her dog has wandered off to, or that she's somebody big. There were a couple of other touches, just to round the image off. One was an ankle bracelet Mom got at a thrift shop, the other was me wearing shoes with a heel to them. Are you getting the idea? Here was this Jolene, coming into class around Halloween, wearing this Lolita outfit, milk-white like she'd been kept indoors since the cradle, and nobody knew what to make of her, me, so they didn't make anything. Like Mom said, I was invisible. They had nothing to compare me to, so they didn't compare. I was the kid from somewhere else.

After that, it was only a matter of mentioning a couple of words to my teacher in a loud voice, words like audition, tests, script, and then, on the playground, asking interested questions like What is kick ball? and What's a fire drill?

Then, out there in Pass-of-the-Camels Park, in the westernmost part of the state, I could go right on about my business. Which was, then as now, attracting as little attention as possible.

23

*O*N THE SEMI-OPULENT aqua and gold ground floor suite at La Fonda Sur Rosa, Glenna and Brogan are dressed straight out of "Dallas." You can almost see the cameras cutting in for closeups.

She's reeking of Shalimar, the perfume she used to wear

when she and Brogan were dating, and has on pencil-thin heels and a black suit with the new short skirt and gold metallic-cloth lapels. Her hair is in a lot of stand-up gold curls, and worn open and almost to her ankles is the Joie de Beavre fur.

Brogan you can hardly recognize. He's got on this Bobby Ewing hairpiece called Alternative Natural Hair Addition and you honestly can't tell it isn't his. Where before he had that kind of bird nest that he was always patting to be sure was still there, this is thick hair that's brushed to the side all loose and natural. Along with the hair he's got a new gesture—I guess the Natural Addition freed up one hand—in which he grabs his chin in a thoughtful way. Definitely terrific how you believe what he says, where before you thought he was maybe bluffing. Now he looks like he thinks maybe *you're* the one who's bluffing, that maybe *your* check is the rubber check. Amazing.

Before everybody arrives, he takes his hairpiece off to show me. It's about a zillion pieces of matching hairs threaded through this see-through plastic "scalp" that, as near as I can tell, is Velcroed right onto his head.

He jumps around to show me how it stays put.

"Even when he's active," Glenna says, "it doesn't budge."

And I know that means they gave it a heavy-screw test the night before.

.   .   .

Suddenly all at once men flood through the door, shaking hands with Brogan and heading for the bar. Those who spot Glenna sitting on the arm of a chair with her legs showing and the fur dragging the carpet get a peck if they've met her before, and if they really know her get a hug as well. The drop-ins and words-of-mouths and friends of friends nod at faces across the room to look like they belong, and Brogan shakes, claps, or nudges them all, because today's crasher is tomorrow's client.

The ones he knows are introduced to me, and the Model thing is working fine. I'm dressed in black with a lot of eye makeup and have moussed my hair so that it looks like early Farrah Fawcett. Exactly what guys think a model should look like. And I have on heels, too, because models are supposed to hit the six-foot mark. My mouth has got a lot of gloss and I don't wear any jewelry—as if I'm on assignment. I'm completely into it, so that every time Brogan says, "You remember Jolene, our little niece, well I guess she's not so little any more, now that she's taken to being a fashion model, ha ha," I hold out my hand and give them a knuckle-cracking shake.

The rancher types all think that's great; you can tell. They all have some fantasy about a model. Maybe the buckets of money they think girls make, or the centerfold idea, something. I can see their minds supplying lots of details, and that's fine. I'm on stage.

L.W. comes in after about half an hour and gives me a salute. Rather, gives me what a stockbroker would think was a high sign. Then, with a quick smile, looking like maybe he has overdressed for this crowd, he unbuttons his vest and loosens his silk tie. Perfect. He's a pro.

Everybody gets a drink and then crowds around a table with an aqua cloth, courtesy of the motel, to munch on ribletts and surimi crab-claw analogs.

Across from the food, on another table, is this giant display that Brogan has rigged up of a cellular phone made to look like a gun. He saw in the paper a couple of weeks ago a picture of a couple of Arabs on the East Coast trying to sell the phone company on the idea, and mocked one up for himself. For this party. It doesn't actually work, and he thinks it may be illegal, but it's an instant stopper.

The men (and now there is a small group of women, too,

in low-necked cocktail dresses and dangling earrings) all have to pick up the gun phone and put it to their ear, their head, point it at each other, then break into belly laughs.

Below the display, Glenna has hand-typed about fifty sheets of paper where the customers can sign up at the bottom if they are interested in seeing a demonstration of the gun phone when it's actually operative. SIGN HERE FOR GUN-PHONE DEMO a big sign says, propped against a quart of Jack Daniel's.

Everybody signs. Some of them sign up partners who can't be there, or bankers they know will take it as a joke, oil prices being what they are, or maybe enemies that they think will fall over dead at somebody walking into their office with this black gun thing.

It's a real conversation piece. The *pee-say dee resistance*, Glenna says.

And, except for the demo, Brogan is not doing any selling. No cookie king flyers; no cocoa photos. He's acting like he's having a big time giving a party—no expense spared, only the best—for all his good clients. Maybe he's going to deduct the party on his income tax, but nobody faults that. The main thing is that nobody feels pressured. Nobody feels that this is in any way a squeeze. So they all relax and get another double and talk about the subject dearest to their hearts: the mess Texas is in.

"Great party, Brog," someone says. "I've had four fingers and nobody's breathed a word about Chapter Eleven for five minutes."

A man in a plaid jacket says, "The only thing in this state that's making money is cul-chure."

"You taking ballet?" Brogan asks, to loud guffaws.

"Houston, let me give you an example, is paying one bunch of million dollars to bring down two hundred and fifty pictures of that hotshot Wyeth's girl friend."

"If I painted two hundred and fifty pictures of some naked

little lady my wife would cut off my hand to the elbow," says a fat man next to him.

"That's not all she'd cut—"

"I mean second, she would." More guffaws.

"Let me tell you about Fort Worth, another example here. Fort Worth, Texas, has got a several-million-dollar campaign to fix up their stockyards. Make them into the Williamsburg of the West."

"I heard Williamsburg was itching to be the Cowtown of the East."

"I heard Fort Worth got the new paper-money plant instead of Dallas."

"Little d could use some of that mint green about now."

"What I want to know is," says the man in the plaid jacket, "what's San Antone doing?"

"I'll tell you what San Antonio, the third largest city in the third largest state in this U.S. of A., is doing—"

"You're behind a census. Make that the second largest of the second largest."

"—in exactly twelve months' time we'll be home to a brand-new Sea World, that's what."

"That's not culture, that's tourism."

"In six months we're going major league with a domed stadium."

"That's not culture, that's sports."

"That's not sports, that's hearsay."

"What about the fifty-three-million-dollar HemisFair Plaza hotel complex, what do you call that?"

"Real estate."

"A scam."

"I'll tell you what San Antone is doing for culture," says the fat man. "It's building a six-million-dollar Fern Barn. Don't laugh. We're talking about connecting your Botanical Gardens to a fifty-foot palm house plus a sunken room for tropicals, plus a free-form reflecting pool, plus the whole shebang which is architect-designed and trapezoid-shaped out of your glass and metal, is going to be partially underground. Now that's *culture*. While little d Dallas is busy getting itself a few more busted banks, our town here is acquiring for itself a one-of-a-cultural-kind commodity."

A silence falls. Nobody knows what to say to that. A Fern Barn?

Brogan decides it's time to bring out his wad of twenties and riffle the folded stack, and he does. Peeling off two without looking and pressing them into the hand of a waiter who walks by carrying a fresh bucket of ice.

. . .

I get a glass of soda and steal a glimpse in the mirror over the aqua sectional sofa. It takes me a minute to recognize myself, and that's good. Behind me I see L.W. and give him a smile, but he's listening for all he's worth to some entrepreneur talking about fire ant eradication.

"Fire ants . . ." The guy begins what sounds like a canned pitch. He's dressed in a shiny suit and has a razor-thin mustache. He looks like the kind of fall guy in films that you know is going to break down and spill everything when the gang gets to him.

"Fire ants are like fleas and roaches, boy. We're not going to rid the world of fire ants. They'll probably be around longer than you and me. But for your pasture and rangeland, even your vegetable garden, my product is fire ant specific. It has very little effect on native ants, all right? No effect whatsoever on honey bees. It also, let me say, has no effect, guaranteed, on aquatics or mammals. Your dogs and cats, mammals. We think we're innovative with this product that has a half-life of thirty years and works up to ten years. Now eighty pounds per acre broadcast of the product will reduce the population immediately, the effective population, as you'll perceive in one minute. You interested in this?"

"It sounds like a good investment to me, sir."

"Investors are what we need. Let me explain to you the way it works. You know your old worker ants are the ones who forage out to feed the colony. Well, we have developed these defatted grits impregnated with soy oil—that's the attractant—and then our insect growth regulator is imbedded in that. No worker ants develop. Got it? We're not *killing* fire ants, we're just zinging them right straight up into the flying stage. Growing them up in a hurry. You apply this growth regulator in the fall and spring, and before the ants go into hibernation they grow wings and fly off and your colony deteriorates. Only one problem, sonny. Flooding. If your application becomes too wet you can forget it: the grits become hush puppy mix."

"That's an amazing product you've got there." L.W. looks as if he's considering cash flow.

"You can say that again." The sleazy man, being an experienced salesman, waits for the other guy to think it over out loud.

"I'm in investments," L.W. tells him. "But these days, I guess you understand, I'm playing it cautious." Slicking down his hair and checking his tie, he says, "Just about the time I began to get the hang of the market, and figure out that a fellow on his toes could make an unobtrusive dollar, the fat hit the fan and insider-trading became a dirty word."

I grin at him across a sea of shoulders, and turn to mingle with the women, who are all bunched up together in a corner.

"Hi." I squeeze into the small circle where they're talking about what a bunch of ape shit horses asses the men are.

"This is too rough for your ears, honey," one of them, a redhead in rhinestone glasses, says to me companionably.

"She's their niece," a big busty blonde explains.

"She's just Brogan's niece. She's not the niece of every limp dick in the place, is she?"

"I didn't ask the exact pedigree."

"I'm Jolene Temple." I give each of the five women a big handshake, which makes them feel better. A big hard squeezer.

"Growing up in this kind of environment will stunt your growth," the redhead warns me.

"Must not have." The blonde gestures, indicating that I'm as tall as she is and then some.

"Tell us about yourself, honey. You were nice to come keep us company. Not your fault how these things go. Women in positions of ownership aren't exactly welcome around here."

"I think we ought to stick together," I tell them. "We women." I look around at the group, and see that they are interested. "My mom and I used to go to this diner run by a fat man named Pete who served the best biscuits west of Natchez and cheese grits with sausage that would make your mouth . . ." I've just got to the punch line and checked to be sure they're all following me when I say, "Eat here or we'll both starve," when I notice this certain man whose back is turned to me.

My voice trails off, although the women seem to like my story and pick it up and begin to toss it around, talking about how the goddamn truth it is.

He's standing by Glenna's side, and at first I think he's talking to her but then I see that he isn't talking to anybody; his shoulder is aimed over her head and he's facing the Sub Rosa's idea of wall art.

The way he stands—rocking back and forth on his heels— reminds me of someone. And even though I don't recognize the suit or even the thick head of brushed-back "Miami Vice" hair, something about him has an awful familiarity.

For a minute I hope I'm wrong. But then I get a sinking

feeling. Because if Brogan can have his Alternative Hair Addition on then there's no reason Turk Jackson can't Velcro one on his head, too. Because that's who I'm looking at, no doubt about it.

Glenna never tumbles, because she's working full time, watching traffic at the gun-phone table, being hostessy, eyeing the room, making sure the Mr. Jack and the roll of twenties are flowing as planned.

Dad turns and finds me looking at him. Since he can't give me a wink because he's wearing shades, he just nods his head and shoots me that sad-looking smile, the smile of a man who's doing his duty, who's come to take me back and provide me with a normal life.

I head toward the bar, edging slowly, keeping a lot of suits and bomber jackets between us. There's a door into the bedroom part of the suite, and I'm thinking that I'll cut out that way.

But when I get almost there, I nearly trip over a thin white waiter who's got a tray full of glasses. He's holding the tray with one hand, sloshing whiskey everywhere, and with the other he holds up two fingers—and nods "his" head toward the bedroom.

I look again at the face, and see, even with the tight man's wig, that, of course, it's Mom. Mom doing her number right under Brogan's nose. Right here in the middle of his March 2, Texas Independence Day, party for customers.

I look around to see if my folks see each other. Mom has spotted Dad, but he hasn't seen her. The usual.

She waves the fingers at me again, and jerks her head to let me know we're going to slip right out through the door I was headed for.

My feet freeze. I look around for L.W., but there's no way I can explain it to him in time. How my parents could be here and nobody know it; how their being here is the absolute worst.

There's only one thing to do and I do it.

Running out the door, down the hall, and through the glittery gold and aqua lobby, I get in my car and head for the only safe place in the world I know.

Henry's studio.

24

W HEN I FIRST started posing for Henry, I thought we would probably fall in love. Then it seemed that as soon as I moved in with him, it was his turn to have that idea.

That first morning when he came in and found me here, half asleep, I was afraid he'd be mad. But he went straight to the kitchen, which is right by the still-life table, with me tagging along behind, and dumped some flour and peanut oil and buttermilk and ice in a bowl, with some salt and baking powder, and before the coffee had even dripped through he had made us hot biscuits. This was before he asked what I was doing here or how I got in.

And even after Henry arrived, the studio didn't look like a studio at all. It looked like what it was when he wasn't working: an ordinary house on an ordinary street. Before he rolled his easel out of the closet-cabinet where he locked it up for the night, in case thieves broke in, you couldn't tell it was a place where anyone painted. If you'd come in the double front doors, through the big tiled room where all the western stuff is, and wandered back to the glass-walled room, all you'd think is that some furniture hadn't arrived or maybe that it was off getting slipcovers. It was the same thing as if Mom had rolled her piano behind a secret panel when she finished her last lesson for the day, and let the split-level ranch pass for any other like it on the street in a neighborhood of similar streets. Safe. That's how it felt that first morning—that the studio wasn't really a studio after all, but just a place where you could sleep late while someone was fixing you breakfast.

As soon as I got here and had pulled the Buick around back so it didn't show from the street, and let myself in with the key that Henry keeps under the edge of what once was a stone birdbath, I called the Sub Rosa and left a message for Glenna.

> Aunt Glenna—
> Mom and Dad showed up at the party.
> I've gone to stay with a modeling friend for a couple of days.
> Don't worry. I'm okay.
>
> —Jolene

I was sure that my leaving wasn't going to be any problem. She and Brogan were used to my disappearing over the years, and I knew they wouldn't send the police looking for me if I left them any kind of message at all. I also knew that they'd probably never tumble to the fact that Mom and Dad were there unless they got my note. Then Glenna would look around the suite and get really mad. She'd tell Brogan later, and they'd lie awake and talk about Midge and Turk and how they never gave up, did they, and then they'd get back to talking about the customers' party.

I didn't do anything about L.W., and still haven't, but I need to do something. A couple of times I was going to call him, later that night, and again the next morning, but there was Henry with the biscuits. And then there was Henry wanting to make love, under the covers, with the crumbs and plates

all around, and me in a shirt and some shorts of his. Wanting
to make love straight style with him on top and a pillow under
my hips as if, I don't know, as if it was the wedding night of
some nervous couple. And he had a big time. He would come
and then step back and arrange the bed and pillows and plates,
leaving a little bit of honey oozing onto the sheets. Then he
tied a ribbon on my hair and called me Sugar, and came again
the same way.

It was really a nice time.

Later, Henry got around to asking me what was going on,
why was I here. But he asked in a natural way, as if he was
asking about the weather, and I told him everything. And
what I noticed while I was talking was that it was okay to
do that, tell him everything that had ever happened with
Mom and Dad, and how they'd showed up at the party,
without even stopping to think about whether I should or
how to say it.

And even while I was telling him, in the back of my mind
I was remembering saying to L.W. that my parents were separated, when he'd asked why I wasn't living with them, that
their jobs took them out of town.

I realized listening to myself tell Henry everything that I
could never have told L.W. the business about Chillicothe or
the stealing me back and forth from playgrounds and class-
rooms. And I was not sure why. I kept asking in the back of
my mind: why? But some things you just know. I could have
said to Henry that my dad had escaped from the pen at
Huntsville. Or that my mom had been picked up for (what
do they call it in the paper?) vagrancy. And not been bothered
telling him.

But I didn't know why that was so. You would think that
somebody with a mother like Henry's and a house that looks
like a museum full of precious furniture would be harder to
tell things to than someone whose mother irons in the living

room, but that wasn't so. Because someone whose mother irons in the living room and whose house is lined in tan everything from top to bottom, you know they can't handle anything weird.

You know they're looking out the window (the window of their mind), peeking through the curtains, afraid they're going to see something weird and not know how to handle it.

I even thought that L.W. felt that me tucking my red panties under his pillow was weird, just a little, and my reaching so fast for his belt. And at the time I was telling Henry about Mom and Dad, and the ongoing phone calls and postcards and fights to see who owned Jolene this week, at the same time I was wondering how a non-weird person would have had sex with L.W. on that single bed on Rosewood under the baseball glove and what she would have done.

What would the Niece do—after she let the chocolate chips cool, and everybody had said yum and had another, chewy but crisp—when it was time to have the love scene, center stage, so that the ironing might continue under dim lights and the calculating intercalary days, also. How that love scene would be played. Probably she, the Niece, would say, I've never done this before, and then Buddy would take her, thump, solid and quick as a good catch, and he'd feel like a real man and she'd begin to cry.

For sure she wouldn't begin, with the sheet wrapped around her and crumbs from a wonderful hot biscuit all buttery and messy still sticking to her lips, to tell him everything there was to tell about renting the furniture for a piano teacher's living room and charging the guest soaps at Sears, or the Terminix "man" holding up three fingers and the white waiter holding up two, or dissolve into laughter about how really awful it was, being in the middle of the tug-of-war between Mom and Dad.

In spite of that, or anyway, I was feeling a little bit guilty about L.W. The thing was I'd invited him to that party, and he was a really good sport and came, all dressed up in his broker suit, and talked to the sleaze about the fire ants, and did a swell job, and then I'd disappeared. It seemed like a bad trick on him, and was not the way I had intended it to be after the party. I thought that after Brogan's cellular phone people left we'd go out for scrambled eggs and bacon, maybe to the diner on San Pedro if it was open, or maybe some nice place on Broadway, the all-night kind where they serve butterscotch pie with whipped cream on top and chopped pecans, that kind of place, and talk about what a help he'd been. And hold hands. After all, we *had* done it, even if his mom and the Pal did come hurrying into the house together to check out what was going on.

But then when Mom and Dad showed up it was the way it is when the lights come up and the curtain goes down and you realize that the scenes lasted too long and the acting wasn't that good, that you paid too much for the tickets, that you've run out of things to say to your date, that you have to go to the bathroom, that your feet hurt, that the car has a flat tire, that your wallet has been lifted—in other words, that the play is over and it's reality time.

Besides. What do you say to somebody normal when your folks catch up with you?

I was afraid maybe Henry was ready for me to pose, and that the talking was over, the way the making love is when he's ready to start painting. But he didn't seem to be in a hurry. I decided that maybe he came in early every morning and sat around for a couple of hours getting himself ready to begin.

"What can I tell L.W. ?" I asked him.

"The actor."

"Yes. He was sort of my date at the party."

Henry washed the bowl and pan, automatically without

thinking about it, and then poured us each some orange juice into paper cups. "Tell him that—" he fixed us back on the bed like a married couple leaning on a pile of pillows having a little chat after sex. "That, umm, an old lover, someone who took advantage of you when you were very young, showed up and that you were scared. That you didn't want your aunt and uncle to find out. That it's some horrid secret from your past he mustn't ask about."

I giggled a little, because what he said sounded absolutely right. Like something you could almost say out loud in the living room on Rosewood with the Dawsons listening.

And then I knew clear as day how the love scene would be played. While Mom pressed pleats and Dad began a month with Sunday, the Niece would say to Buddy, I can't, not yet, not now, there is some terrible trauma in my past. I was hardly more than a child. Please don't ask, oh, please, don't make me tell. And he would hold her tight Under Brown Umbrella as the lights dimmed.

25

TODAY HENRY MAKES more biscuits and we eat them again on the bed. I posed until late last night, and we slept without moving until the sun came up.

It turns out Henry stays here most nights during the week; on the weekend he stays at the fancy house unless he tells his mother he's not coming. March 2 was really a Monday, but Brogan had his party on a Sunday night, and that's why Henry wasn't here when I came.

"What did they do after you left?" he asks now, wiping a crumb off my chin.

"Who?" I'm not following him, being busy trying to wake up and feeling a little stiff from standing still so long last night.

"Mom and Dad."

"At the party, you mean? I don't know. I told you—"

"What do you suppose they did? Picture it."

I think about that and decide that Dad never does find out that Mom is also there; that she sees him, and sees me leave, and drops her tray and heads for the bedroom of the suite, thinking I'll be waiting in there. And after a while she doesn't believe it when I don't show up, and pokes her head back in where the party is, and then sneaks around in there and goes down the hall, still expecting to see me. And then? I don't know. I never ran away before.

Dad? He maybe confides to Brogan that under the new hair it's him, Turk, talking to Brogan under his new hair. And Brogan doesn't punch him in the nose for showing up, because of the good old boy customers, but he'd like to, and he signals Glenna with his eyes and maybe a finger pointing, but she's already got my note, so she knows, and she can't believe she's been in the same room with Turk Jackson, right under his nose in her Joie de Beavre, and she could kick herself. She shows Brogan the note and they tell Dad I'm not there. But Dad probably stays on anyway and puts the party to bed. He's like that. Being a salesman to the soles of his feet, he probably sold a few oil rig supplies to the same men Brogan was feeding, sold oil rig supplies at a time when people weren't even pumping mud from their so-called dry-bed navigable streams, much less oil from their back forties. But Dad is like Mom: he could sell oil to the Arabs.

So I tell Henry that.

Then he asks, "What would they have done if you'd stayed?"

"You mean if I'd left with Mom?"

"If you'd gone on about the business of the party. Talking to the women ranchers. When your mom held up two fingers, what would she have done if you'd paid no attention, or if you'd taken a drink from her tray and told her thanks?"

The very idea sends goose bumps along my arms, and I burrow back down under the covers. I can't imagine that. Me, pay no attention? The Terminix "man" in the hall, and me walk right into Mrs. Evans's classroom and pick up my pencil for long division? Me wave and mention that there were a lot of roaches in the custodian's closet? Not possible. "Some things are not possible," I tell Henry.

"What would have happened if you'd said, 'Hi, Dad, good to see you, you're looking well, Mom's over there helping out at the bar. I'll tell my uncle you're here.' "

I completely cover my head. The idea is terrifying. Henry lifts off the quilt and asks, "What? What would have happened?"

I scoot down until I'm about at his knees. It's one of those things that is like a roller coaster ride or a horror movie, to ask yourself how it would be if you did something that you never did and couldn't ever do in a million years. He doesn't understand about needing to hide.

"You don't understand," I tell his kneecaps.

He pulls me back up. "That's where you're wrong."

He brings us some hot cocoa in mugs I haven't seen before that say HIS and HERS and have some kind of silly overalls on one and a pinafore on the other. I cannot imagine these belonging to Henry.

"What?" he asks again.

I shake my head.

"Mom's holding up three fingers."

"Two. It was two for March second."

"Two." He demonstrates.

I close my eyes.

"Dad's got on dark glasses."

I cover my ears.

Henry kisses my eyelids. "Let me tell you," he says. "Let me tell you about what happens."

He gets up out of bed and pulls on his drawstring pants and a faded blue shirt. He looks sleepy, too, and younger than usual, although I know he must be nearly forty-five. He must be. He is tall and loose and his bones seem too big for his skin, if that makes sense. He has what you think of as a European face, all those eye sockets and jawbones and skull bones and collarbones. I imagine he was considered handsome when he was young. He must have been to have had two wives. And that seems strange to me just now, with Henry playing His and Hers in the bedroom in a honeymoon sort of way, the idea of him doing all this seriously, standing up there and getting married, having a real honeymoon, talking about dishes and towels and all that stuff. It doesn't seem believable. Maybe he had very European marriages, whatever they would be. Married on top of a mountain and then skiing down, or out in a meadow and then riding off on horseback? Now I laugh out loud, and that makes me feel better.

. . .

Henry has a box when he comes back. He motions me to come to the still-life table, and we pull up chairs. While he talks, he holds the box, which is tied up with a string, in one hand, keeping the other hand on my back.

"When I was a kid," he says, "my mother went by the name of Kraft. I thought that was our name. She said my daddy had died in the war, and she had a picture of a man in uniform. It wasn't my daddy, it was just a photo she'd found. She was ashamed of my daddy. He could hardly read and write. His people weren't educated. They worked ranches, they worked horses. She was ashamed that she'd run off and married him."

"Your mother?" The tiny lady in floating gray who was too good for everybody on earth?

"She took me and ran away from him, left him, and went out to Colorado, where she had cousins. She told them some story—they weren't close—took the name of Kraft, went to school, and got a job as a receptionist in a doctor's office where she could watch the patients and pick up the way they talked and acted. She got rid of every trace of hill country rancher's ways."

"I thought ranchers had money." I'm thinking of Brogan's clients, or the ones he wishes were clients.

"Big West Texas ranches, yes. Small rocky spreads in the hill country? Not back then. They had absentee owners, and he was essentially just a hand; he was a hand. For a while he tried other jobs but they never lasted. He knew how to work ranches and that's what he always went back to."

"Did you ever meet him?"

"When I was almost grown."

He opens the box and takes out a packet of letters. He spreads open the first three for me, flat on the table by the vase of daisies.

They are handwritten on lined notepad paper and hard to read. The spelling isn't good and there are capital letters where they shouldn't be. It would be too insulting to give all the mistakes, but I'll just give the idea, because they make me want to cry.

Dear Bess,

How do you and the boy like your new home. Has he started to school yet. Tell him I feed Kitty Cat when she comes around.

Mailing you each $1.00 to buy anything you want.

Red

Dear Bess,

How are you and the boy getting along. Are you playing in the Snow. Don't let the Bear bite you. I clipped a bunch of hair at the end of Blue's tail and am going to find some Rabbits for him to run. I built a Flower Box across the porch. Mailing you each $5.00. Buy what ever you want. If you want to buy some Steaks or Pork Chops or what ever do it.

Red

Dear Bess,

Its 12:20 am. Working 11–7. Will draw $72 through Dec. 5, $62.50 through Dec. 19 and that's all. Be sure and watch the Antifreeze in the car. Will pack up Xmas Decorations you like and send them by bus. How does the boy like school. Will send some money soon.

Red

I smooth the letters out and read them again. It makes me think a lot of things about Henry that I didn't think before. Makes me understand why he doesn't get mad at his mother, and then it makes me wonder why he doesn't get really mad at her and never see her again.

I hand him his daddy's letters.

He folds the lined pages and puts them back in the stack. "I have some letters from my uncle, a few."

"To his mistress?"

"To my daddy, but my daddy couldn't read them, more than likely. It was a big family, eight children. My uncle ran off as a boy and bought himself a camera. The rest of them went to work; they thought he was crazy."

"Why didn't he ever marry the woman with the hand?"

Henry takes my hair and turns my face so he's kissing my throat. "Marriage, as you'll find out, hasn't got much to do with what matters."

"Are you talking about your wives?"

He pulls my chair over to his and keeps on holding on to my hair with one hand and the box with the other. "The first one married my mother's house; the second married my gallery openings. I gave the first one a big piece of what she wanted, and the second one a fair share of sales."

"But what made you marry them, then?"

He tugs me closer. "Wozencrantz was just getting used to himself. Henry Kraft, a miserable skinny kid with knobby knees and too much hair, didn't know how to say no to Beauty propositioning."

I think about what that means.

He puts the letters in the box. "When I got to high school, I pressed my mother about the family. I asked my cousins, who didn't know much, but some. I made a trip back to Texas and asked around the hill country. It's a small world up there with no secrets. Everybody knew somebody who knew Red Wozencrantz. The main thing was I'd found out the name; I'd pried it out of her."

"When did you start to go by your daddy's name?"

"When I began to paint. I'd heard the name Wozencrantz, because there weren't many artists being recognized in our part of the world. Not but a handful with his reputation. But I hadn't known—how could I?—that he was my uncle. It was a revelation. To think that a family like his, as it turned out my family, too, had produced him. Or, more accurately, hadn't stopped him. When I learned of the connection, I went around to see him; introduced myself. It was *his* name I wanted, my uncle's. It was his name I used." He seems to be back a long time ago. "Later, when I started to show, it helped."

He tugs my hair a minute. "I've spent thirty years of my life, you might say, making ours a name my mother can be proud of. I tried to show her that if you get big enough, they can't get to you any more."

"She uses your name."

"When enough people recognized it, she took it back. But it's only veneer. Inside, she still denies it. She spent her life running away, and she's running still."

"You're talking about Mom and Dad and me, aren't you?"

"More or less."

"I guess you're saying that I should go back to Brogan and Glenna's. That my folks can't get me if I don't let them." I don't believe that for a minute, but I get the idea that he's ready to stop all the talk, and is leading up to telling me that he's through now with the old letters, the HIS and HERS cups, and biscuit crumbs, and is ready to roll his easel out of the cabinet and get to work.

"I'm saying something else. I'm saying that sooner than you're ready for it you won't have this problem ever again. You may have other problems, and you may hate the sight of me—more than likely you will—but you won't have this particular problem again."

"I don't understand."

"You're not to, not yet. I'm saying stay here, Jolene. Stay as long as you want. This is more than I'd hoped for, to have you here. The bed, the table, the studio, all of it was made for you." He pushes back his chair. "I thought you'd never come."

And with that, while I am still trying to figure out what he means, and if he is joking with me or not, he pulls me up and leads me back to the bed. "Was there ever a time in my life I didn't love you?" he asks, as he takes off his clothes and buries himself in me.

26

I DECIDE that if Henry is really painting while we're doing it and doing it while we're painting, then what I'm doing while I'm posing is running away.

I wish I could just leave Brogan and Glenna a note saying: Thanks a couple of million times for everything, but right now I'm hiding out in this two-story room with lots of good glare. Drop me a note when the coast is clear. I'll come back to see you sometime—when I'm about thirty.

Plus I'm glad the big party for all the bankrupt ranchers turned out fine.

27

I CHECK with Glenna that the coast is clear before I show up. I don't have any idea what Mom and Dad may do. The times they've shown up in the same place before, that I know about at least, were the times, naturally, when one of them had me and the other came slipping around to take me back.

I guess I'm going back to Glenna's now not just to pick up a few things but to see how it feels to be back with family.

On the one hand, I feel safer at Henry's than I've ever felt in my life, but on the other I'm worried that he's changing how he treats me.

We had a fight about that today.

We've been talking a lot, not deep stuff all the time, just talk. This morning he made cocoa and brought it in those HIS and HERS mugs. We made a joke about where were the marshmallows and didn't I have any pajamas with feet in them.

I got to talking about how I'm the youngest in my family, and always will be, even when I'm walking around with a cane or pedaling an old folks' go-cart. That's because Brogan and Glenna couldn't have kids, and Mom had only me. (Dad, too, I guess, at least as far as I know.) Henry said, no, that that would change when I had kids, but I told him I thought I'd skip that part.

Then Henry said he was the oldest in his family or would be when his mother was gone, and always would be because obviously nobody could come along and be older. He said the generation he's in has already bred like rabbits, so that the next one down, his daughter's generation, is sure to multiply like the leaves on the trees, he said, or the hairs on our heads or the cars on the freeway.

He said that all of them focused up on him; and I said all of my folks focused down on me.

I told him we were like an hourglass, the two of us; that we were the part where the sand ran through, me at the place where the glass points down and him at the place where it points up. And he liked that, and drew a little cocoa hourglass on his chest.

Later, when it was time to start posing, I said I was going to write L.W. exactly what he told me to. I thought he'd be pleased, but he wasn't.

"I don't want you seeing that boy while you're living here."

"L.W.? But I'm going to. He was a good sport to come to that party. And then I ran out on him."

"He's an actor."

"I know; I told you that."

"Don't you know actors are grave robbers?" He balanced

his cup with its silly overalls on the palm of his hand in the air. Maybe he was making a stage. "They dig up old bodies. You fuck an actor you don't know who he is. Maybe he's his own grandfather, or he's some man he saw as a kid in the tourist line at the Alamo. He's somebody he read about dead for fifty years. It's necrophilia. You go to bed with an actor, it's necrophilia."

"I was taking acting," I reminded him.

"You were Jolene taking an acting class. Horse of a different color. You have to not exist to be an actor. Nobody in the mirror." He demonstrated by pretending to look at the side of his cup and wipe his hand across it and there's nobody there. It made me laugh.

But I didn't let that business go about seeing L.W. I told Henry that I'd had enough of people prying into my life, that I had a history of that. I wasn't going to have him tell me that I couldn't see somebody I wanted to; I had a history of that, too. People, I explained, who have been a bone for more than a dozen years like me don't get excited when they see a couple of dogs about to fight over them.

Still, I've liked a lot sleeping in that bed with Henry, such a deep sleep in recent nights that I haven't waked up until the sun came flooding through the windows, and even then I sat up and looked around, forgetting where I was. The kind of deep sleep I don't ever remember having before. I think from those early years of living with Mom and Dad, back and forth, I got in the habit of sleeping with one ear open. They say people who have babies do that; maybe people who have parents do it, too.

. . .

As I drive from Henry's to Glenna's—which is actually only a distance of ten blocks off the same north-south street, but neither of them knows that—I begin to get slightly spooked.

It may be I'm just jumpy, but I think there is a red car, a rental-red car, following me. At least it was behind me when I turned onto New Braunfels, and just now it made the same right turn I did. It may be my imagination, a hangover from all those years with Mom suspecting that one of the men, Dad or Brogan, was around every corner or about to appear at every intersection.

At least I hope so.

28

GLENNA GIVES me a big Shalimar-scented hug. She's all excited. Brogan is bringing her good news, he just called, and a present. Something she's been wanting for a long time, he said, but she can't begin to guess what that could be.

She says she doesn't think I need to stay gone, really, that Mom and Dad can't do a thing now that I'm grown. But she seems to understand how I feel, and gives me a second hug before we go out on the patio.

We sit at the wrought iron table the way she and Brogan do on Sundays, and drink a tall thick pineapple milkshake. It's her new diet drink, made with skim milk, fresh pineapple, and lots of crushed ice from her icemaker. She says she's had it up to here with spiced-up tomato juice.

"You doing all right, honey?"

"Fine. I'm modeling a lot, and so that's good. I'm sorry I ran off the way I did. But seeing them again—I guess I just plain panicked."

Glenna looks sympathetic, like she understands. Then she

frowns and, without thinking, runs her finger over the line it makes. "I still don't think your mother was there, although if you say you saw her, you of all people ought to know. But when the motel man handed me your note, I looked everybody over top to bottom. For a minute I asked myself, Glenna Rose, how do you know you'd even know Midge Temple after all this time if she was standing right smack dab in front of you, but the thing is you do; you can't call up a person's face on the spur of the moment, but as soon as you see it, you know.

"It was that way with your father. It was that way with Turk. He must have been right there in front of my nose in plain sight, but we had a lot of drop-ins and Brogan was concentrating on signing up his regulars, so I wasn't paying the off-chances much attention. I looked around as soon as I read your note, but he must have ducked out right on your heels. Then about a half an hour later there he was, and even in that fancy new hairpiece, I knew it was him, no doubt about it. To tell the truth—now you mustn't get mad—he was a help at the party." She checked out my reaction. "Going around the way he does, shaking hands. Like he was part owner of the business. Even Brogan said he had a lot of nerve, but he had to admit Turk was a help. Under different circumstances, you know, I bet those two would really get along. That's not something I ever thought before. Sometimes something like that just hits you. You look at people you've known for a coon's age, and it's like you'd just seen them new for the first time. Looking at Brogan and your daddy I thought, Why, those two men could be best friends—if things had worked out differently."

Aunt Glenna made a little face when she said "differently," not wanting (Glenna is always careful about that) to say anything directly derogatory about Mom. I don't think that's because Mom is Brogan's sister, because Glenna can sometimes get in a few remarks about Hoyt and Cissy, his parents, but because Mom is my mother, and Glenna doesn't think it's nice to run down my natural mother. Because maybe that implies that I haven't turned out so well; because if I turned out well, then Mom must have had something to do with that. I've heard her say that to Brogan and Cissy, defending Mom, when one of them was up in arms about Midge attempting to run off with me again.

But maybe that isn't the real reason; maybe the real reason is that if Mom hadn't been the way she is, then Glenna would never have ended up with me—and I'm the nearest thing to a daughter she has.

I tell her that the pineapple shake is her best invention yet, and we have a small refill and are just wiping our mouths when we hear Brogan's Olds roar into the driveway.

. . .

"We're cased on coverall," he says, waving a stack of papers in the air.

"Don't speak to me in that foreign language."

"Just your bingo lingo," he says, giving us each a kiss on the cheek and pulling out a chair for himself. "Now, you remember the table we had set up at our customers' party at the La Fonda Sur Rosa?"

"At the party? What table?"

"That table. At the party. With the gun-phone display and the sheets of paper on which we got exactly fifty-five genuine signatures."

"Brogan Temple, you haven't been actually placing orders for that come-on have you?"

"That display was more than a come-on; it was a coup." He waves the pieces of paper in her face.

"Where have you been with those?"

"Made a couple of necessary stops. Numero Uno, I went to Jiffy Copy and had a short contract printed up on the top of every page, right above that form for name and address."

"That's dishonest."

"Nothing crooked, the whole thing was aboveboard. I didn't even have to misrepresent the facts." He leans over until he is about six inches from her face. "Now, here's what I did. Here's what happened. I went into the bank with the signatures as collateral you might say, fifty-five authentic names and addresses of persons interested in a product that I just might be marketing. All right? Now. I'm waving these, but I'm not making a lot out of them, see? I sit down on the customer side of the loan officer's desk at the bank and I say, 'I want to branch out.' 'Don't we all,' he says. 'Some want to branch out and some want to bail out.' And then we take time out to have a good laugh at his joke, which he's making a note to remember so he can tell it again to the vice-president in the men's room. Then I confide to him—still holding my signatures but not pressing them on him, not making any reference to them—I confide to him that the coming thing is vineyards."

"Vineyards?" Glenna knits her brow, trying to follow.

"The same thing he said. 'Vineyards?' I told him, 'Even The University of Big Texas has turned its bunch of millions from oil to grapes.' Then I reminded him that the High Plains of West Texas is a viticultural Promised Land, and then—this is the hooker—I asked him, what does he think California was but an earthquake about to happen before they got the brilliant idea of California wines?

"He thought about that. He was about a dozen years younger than yours truly, razor cut, buttoned vest, and he was dazed at the concept. He didn't have a glimmer until that moment that there had ever been a California without wines. Then he had to consider, and you could see the wheels in his head go around, he had to sit there in his Hart Schaffner & Marx and wish real bad that his granddaddy, who never amounted to a hill of beans, had been out there buying grape-vines when they were going cheap.

"While he locomoted his brain cells, I added a few backup facts. Such as the fourteen varieties of native grapes and the four thousand acres already planted, and that if it'd been the French instead of the Pentecostals settling the state, Lubbock would this very minute be the South of France.

" 'How much you need?' he asked me, and I could see he was interested in ferreting out a little more information on the matter, on the sly getting the specifics on exactly where these opportunities for investment existed. So in a semi-casual way I mentioned the fine varietals available right this minute from canny vintners who were beating us to the draw, and I named a few names he was going to recognize right off the bat. Former oil types. Previous politicians. And how these folks were already selling about three-quarters of a million gallons a year, selling their own private little Red *Bor-deaux* or their sweet little *Chen-in Blanc*."

Glenna repeats the French names, impressed with Brogan's unsuspected knowledge.

"So now I've got his attention, the junior loan officer. So I say, 'But first, I need to clear up a little bookkeeping matter with you.' I'm ready to strike my bargain with him, because I can see he's itching for me to leave so he can sprain his finger calling his broker to inquire about the return on investment in vineyards. 'What's that?' he asks, and I tell him, 'There's this little matter of my parents who are right now not happy with your bank, which is playing the heavy with their mort-gage. Hardly an amount of money worth the stamps to send out your Payment Overdue letters, but they're getting up there in years, they have some old movie in their heads about the sheriff coming out on horseback to foreclose.' We have a good laugh at that. Then he says, 'These new people.' He waves away the mortgage department with one buffed pinky. 'They don't know half the ass time what their right hands are doing.'

"So real quick I give him the details, Block 48, Lot 4, nice piece of real estate in the right part of town, and he agrees, 'No problem, Mr. Temple—Brogan, right?—no problem,' to put a temporary balloon note on it, and then we've finished our business for the day. And I never had to say a word about the signed order blanks on the desk lying underneath his nose the entire time."

"How is that going to help when the La Fonda Sur Rosa bill comes due?"

"More than likely we'll be out of town at the time, on business. More than likely we'll have to drop them a note explaining that, temporarily only, our cash flow is tied up in wine futures, that we've gone to check on our holdings."

"If we go out there, can I wear my coat?"

"Can you wear your coat?"

"My Joie de Beavre."

"Sure you can. Tell the grape growers in West Texas you ordered it over your cellular from your Coupe de Ville."

Glenna relaxes at that. "You're nice, you know it, helping out your folks."

"That's me." He enjoys that for a spell and then pats her hand. "But I was about to forget. I just happen to have here a little token, which just happens to be something you've been wanting for a very long time."

"What?" She sees he has a tiny package.

"Guess."

"How can I guess?" She rattles the box, looks all excited. "Can I open it?"

"Your aunt," Brogan says to me, calling on a sympathetic third party, and wanting to draw out the surprise a little

longer, "has on more than one occasion expressed an interest
in having herself an own name."

"What in the world?" She tears at the pink paper and
silver ribbon.

"It so happens that is exactly what your aunt is about to
receive. Compliments of me, your uncle."

Glenna pulls out a gold charm, reads the engraved inscrip-
tion to herself, then reads it aloud with a squeal of delight:
" 'Glenna Rosé'!"

"That'll be the premier wine from our first crush."

"Brogan Temple, you are without a doubt the sweetest
man in the whole world."

It's great to be with them again, with Hoyt and Cissy's
house saved, and Brogan off on another scam, and Glenna
getting a wine named after her (or getting herself renamed
after a wine), and me between them, serving as witness. It
seems like old times.

And sure enough it is.

Just at that moment a big, rental-red car crawls slowly
down the street and pulls to a stop at their house.

29

"SHE'S RIGHT OUT LIVING with a
man old enough to be her father."

"How do you know?"

"How do I know? Because I'm her father, that's how. I
know how old I am."

"That she's living with him."

"I saw with my own eyes. Went in, she did, and as far as I know didn't come back out all night. Next morning he showed up and let himself right in, big as you please."

"Maybe it's a family. Wife and five children."

There's silence. Dad is stuck. I imagine him patting his Velcro; rocking back and forth on his heels. Is he going to admit to Brogan he looked in the windows, or bugged the studio? Did he? Could he? Or is he only guessing?

Glenna and I are standing in her bedroom listening through the door. Henry should be proud of me. Here I came back to pick up my stuff and when that rental-red car pulled right up in the drive, instead of doing my vanishing act, I disappeared into the bedroom. He ought to give me points for that, although I admit I've got my eye on the double windows. The screens look easy as pie to unlatch and the ground is right there three feet down on the side of the house away from Dad's Avis Mercury Marquis.

If he followed me to Henry's the night of the Sub Rosa party, has he been hanging around ever since? The idea that he and Mom are circling again like vultures doesn't make me feel great. (Not that Dad would know that Mom was around; that's where she has the advantage over him.)

Glenna motions me to come sit by her on the bed. It's not as if we have to press our ears to the keyhole. Dad and Brogan can probably be heard across the yard on the patio next door. The dentist's wife is more than likely listening to every word; she's turned down her soaps and is getting the real thing.

"If you're casting aspersions on that fine daughter of yours or making any low-grade cracks about what she's up to, you can get out of my house right this second, Turk Jackson, and that's a genuine threat. A finer girl than that one doesn't walk the streets of the Alamo City."

Dad clears his throat, sort of the way one dog backs down from another. "What you have to take into account, Brog, and here I'm talking man to man, is that it's a new ball game out there."

"What ball game are you talking about? It wasn't paddle tennis in our day."

"I mean sexually speaking. The rumble-seat stuff has gone out the window."

"Did you ever even lay your eyes on a rumble seat even at an auto show? Where'd you ever hear about a rumble seat? Hoyt and Cissy were making out in the back seat of a Pontiac in their day."

"Figuratively speaking."

"So say what you're saying."

"I'd like you to take a look at this packet."

"I'm having sex education in my own living room? My sister's husband is giving *me* sex education? Pardon me, but anyone who married my sister Midge has got a large-size gap in his own sex education if you ask me."

"Brog, give this a look-see."

" 'Safe Sex,' " Brogan reads aloud.

Glenna smothers a laugh. She grabs the blender full of pineapple milkshake and takes a big gulp.

"Safe sex, my heinie, you'll see what I mean," Dad says.

" 'What Is Safe?' " Brogan's voice sounds half an octave deeper, like he's showing that this topic does not in the least bother him, a man like him, of the world.

" 'Masturbation; oral sex on a man using a condom, being sure to avoid the pre-cum . . .' Jesus, Turk, where'd you get this filth?"

"This little packet in the blue plastic envelope was handed to me by your sorority sister with a lot of hair on the campus of our very own state university."

Brogan tries a joke. "For my purposes, I think Glenna and I've pretty well got the thing figured out."

"Keep reading. We're talking about my little daughter who

is right this minute engaging in God knows what with a pervert old enough to be her father."

There is the sound of breathing and a couple of coughs. " 'What's Unsafe?' 'Kissing.' *Kissing?* 'Anal intercourse.' What the hell?"

"Keep going."

" 'Fisting'?" Brogan coughs again.

"Go on."

" 'Rimming'?"

"Keep reading."

" 'Watersports'? Jesus Himself Christ, Turk, this is your homosexual tract you've got here." Brogan's voice cracks. "This calls for three fingers of Mr. Jack, if you ask me."

"I won't say no to that idea, Brog."

We hear glasses and then we don't hear anything for a few minutes. Glenna finishes off the milkshake, to be sociable. She looks shocked but at the same time a little bit thrilled. You can see she wants to ask me what all those things mean and am I really doing them, but then part of her wants to believe that I'm not that kind. I know she and Brogan will sit up half the night reading the pamphlet on Safe Sex and getting themselves excited, or else, more likely, getting themselves sobered up into not feeling like doing it after all.

Then Brogan asks Dad, "Tell me the truth, Turk, do you know what all this stuff is? Do you have any idea what this means? Fisting? What the hell. Do you have any idea what we're talking about here?"

"It's a new ball game, like I told you, Brog. People are dying of doing things that you and me, old-timers, that you and me don't know one little thing about."

"Kissing? *Kissing?* Jerking off is okay but kissing isn't? We didn't see stuff this hard-core in fourth grade, if you know what I mean."

"Now you get my drift, Brog. My little girl has got herself

out there in a world which isn't even a double first cousin once removed to normal any more. Do you see why I want to take her back? Take her somewhere safe?"

"You got a place at the South Pole?"

"She's entitled to a normal life."

"You casting any aspersions on anyone in this house? You suggesting any abnormalities on these premises?"

Dad clears this throat. "A man gets a certain age, he wants his family."

We hear glasses being refilled. Then Brogan uses a calmer tone. "Now I'm going to remind you of a little evening not too long ago, the occasion of a little party of mine for some loyal customers. As I recall you put in an appearance, helped out with the crowd."

"It was a good party."

"That evening, the one under discussion, the young lady we've been talking about had a date with a stockbroker. Do you understand what I'm saying? A stockbroker who right out loud confessed to a customer of mine that he engaged in insider-trading. Now the first thing to remember about his type, the upward mobe, is that he is making it hand over fist and what he doesn't put up his nose he's going to spend on investigating your high-class leisure-time activities, some of which we've just been reading about. Now, don't you just suppose that someone like this, busy with skimming and wristing and loiter-sports is going to do more harm to our girl than some guy as old as we are who's never heard of a one of these newfangled methods and who thinks it's real nice just to put his hand up some lady's skirt? Which would you rather? You've got to take a look at the realistic alternatives."

"You've got a point."

"A man doesn't know what something is, he can't be doing it."

"That makes sense."

"Let me give you a couple more fingers, Turk. For the road."

"I could be persuaded."

"That age, the best thing you can do is hope they got sense."

"She never had a decent home."

"Present location in which you're sitting excepted?"

"No offense. I forget when I get riled up you're next of kin to the girl's mother."

"I forget that myself when I can."

"How're your folks? They must be getting up there."

"Hoyt and Cissy had a recent scrape with the bank, nothing major, a matter of their mortgage on Lot 4, Block 48—"

Dad laughs real loud. "Some things don't change."

"How about checking back with us come summer?" Brogan thinks he's got things smoothed over. "You'll be down this way; things are going to pick up in the oil business, mark my words. If you still want her then, well, me and Glenna, for one, will be willing to reason."

"Kind of you, Brog."

Something about this is beginning to give me the creeps. Dad saying, Some things don't change, rings a bell in my head. Glenna thinks everything is settled and sets her empty blender on the floor and gives me a big hug. Her eyes are wet. And all the time I'm hugging back I'm thinking that this doesn't sound like Dad. Or, rather, that it sounds a whole lot like Dad and I know what that means, even if they don't.

"I guess I'll be on my way," he says. "Thanks for the Mr. Jack."

"Keep in touch."

"Oh, I'll be in touch all right. You'll be the first to get a notification of my whereabouts and those of my daughter who I am as of this minute no longer going to allow to stay in this environment where no telling what has been going on. Living in sin with a man old enough to be her father, and I should know. Plus carrying on with some cocaine-snorting, funds-embezzling stockbroker on the side. You hung yourself, Brog. I heard it from the horse's mouth."

Then, just as he hollers at the top of his lungs, "Come on out here, Jolene, I know you're in there, come on out," I unlatch the screen and follow my suitcase to the ground.

I figure I'll have his rental-red car in my rearview mirror before he's hefted himself up off the couch and turned the knob on the bedroom door.

30

I GOT MY SEX EDUCATION in the Panhandle.

We were on the run again, pulling a U-Haul loaded with our possessions, looking, as always, to widen our horizons. Studying the map at a back-road barbeque stand, Mom considered our options. We had time: no one would think to look on the old highway, now barely a two-lane, plus Dad thought I was at a pep rally and would be for two more hours.

In Honey Grove Hills, Mom recalled, we were a stone's throw from two states, Arkansas and Louisiana. In Pass-of-the-Camels Park, we had quick access to three borders: New Mexico, Mexico, and Arizona.

"Look at this," she said, pointing to Amarillo in the Panhandle, "only a hop, skip, and a tank of gas from four states of the Union: Oklahoma, Colorado, Kansas, and New Mexico." It was too much to pass up.

So we didn't.

Within a day of our arrival, she'd located us a brand-new tract house on Palo Verde Drive ("green wood"), in Tierra Blanca Estates ("white earth"), on the outskirts of Amarillo ("yellow"), only a picnic away from the nearby Red River with its hundred-and-twenty-mile-long gorge.

It was a colorful locale.

Palo Verde, we learned, got its name from the clump of green-barked retama/huisache optimistically planted on every block; Tierra Blanca, from the surrounding mineral-leached, flash flood–bleached acid soil; and the metropolis itself from the yellow flowers on the yellow banks of a nearby yellow lake.

Mom thought we'd found a safe 'burb at last; that we'd come there to stay. The Panhandle, she reasoned, was too far away from civilization for Dad to travel on a hunch. He'd miss too many days' work—and besides, there were more oil rig supply salesmen than oil rigs in that part of the world already.

.   .   .

"What do you want to know about boys?" she asked me one night when I was working on math.

My guard went up. If I answered Nothing, that meant I already knew everything there was to know, and I'd be in deep trouble. If I told her something specific, anything specific, then she would focus on that. I knew what had brought this on: I'd got my period, I was developing breasts. I was scaring her to death. If she could have squeezed me back into four-year-old Sonny's secondhand suit permanently she would have.

What I wanted to know about boys was mostly how to get alone with one without Mom knowing about it. But I knew that wasn't the right thing to say.

"Why?" I asked, having learned that a question was the best answer.

"It's time you were asking."

"Well, I have, some."

"Have *what?*"

"Asked."

"Asked who? You'll get misinformation. You'll get in trouble."

"Asked the boys. I figure they know anything I need to know about boys."

"Give me strength. Give me sustenance." She fixed herself a bowl of cereal. Her hair was up in plastic home-permanent rollers, drying after a shampoo. She thought piano teachers should have body to their hair. She also thought they should wear a lot of navy blue. It was part of the image.

"Men," she started in again, "—boys are only small men— men are all gamblers. That's what you need to know. I'm not interested in discussing the birds and bees, did you think that? Or how to kiss French or when to smack his face, did you think that? I'm talking about the basic personality of the male of the species. They gamble. They gamble for you, then they gamble with you, then they gamble you away."

"You're talking about Granddaddy."

"Tell me something new."

"But not Uncle Brogan—"

"Says you. My brother's life is one big throw of the dice, one big draw to an inside straight."

"Not Dad."

She made a face. "No, not your dad. His only gamble was me. He folded after the first hand."

I did have something on my mind about boys I wanted to know: how Mom happened to get involved with one, namely, how she and Dad had got together. I knew there'd been a time when they seemed in love, but even then they were fighting with each other and tugging at me. (I sometimes imagined the nurse in the hospital showing me to them and both of them making a grab for the kid wrapped in the blanket.)

"I do have a question."

"It's time you were asking."

"Why did you start going with Dad?"

"End of sex education for the semester. It's time for your bath."

"Tell me how you met him."

"How I met Turk Jackson." Mom stood up like she was in front of a class reciting, giving her plastic rollers a little pat. "How I met Turk Jackson was I was some dumb girl who laid eyes on this big lunk with this full head of hair—which he had in those days—and those white teeth flashing like head-lights, and I thought I'd just fall head over heels like a ton of bricks, having nothing else dumb to do that week."

She sat back down, shook out her fingers, and began to play notes in the air, as if she was accompanying herself with a little melody along with her words. "So I did. I said, Here I am, take me, make a mess out of my life. Stomp all over my feelings. Make me promises you're breaking faster than you can make them. So he says, That's just what I had in mind, baby. Stick with me and we'll head down the road to yester-day. Stick with me and we'll be two flat tires on a deserted road without a spare. Stick with me and we'll go nowhere."

She got up, closed the imaginary piano, and took a bow. "I believe that's more or less what we said, your dad and I, in the front seat and the back seat of whatever revved-up auto-mobile he was making late payments on at that time."

"Okay."

"What did you want me to say? We were a match made in heaven but we never got there?"

"I was just asking."

"I was just telling. I'm not going to say it was your fault, for getting born, if that's what you're fishing for, because you had nothing to do with it. If you'd never come along we'd be doing just what we're doing now, which is trying to get even."

I wanted to believe her, but I was not sure I did. "But if you hadn't had me, you wouldn't ever have to see Dad, or hear from him again."

"So maybe that's why the stork flapped her wings over the cabbage patch, did you ever think of that?"

I hadn't, but what she said made me wonder if just once— there on Palo Verde Drive in Tierra Blanca Estates—some truth had accidentally crossed Mom's lips.

31

*H*ENRY IS MAD I'm late.

And that I've come back with only a suitcase. Most of all he's mad I let Dad get me in a frantic state of mind again. And that I let myself out the window and didn't have it out with Dad.

I tell him he doesn't understand. He doesn't understand how it is not to feel safe anywhere at all. He has no idea what it's like to wonder every time I'm out if everybody I pass or anybody I speak to is really Mom or Dad in drag or some new getup.

I tell him how long it took me just to drive back here to his house. That first I drove all up and down every street in the *-wood* section off San Pedro, and then every street in the *-hurst* section, and then hit the subdivision whose streets are named for the flowers of Texas, thinking that if Dad was back there somewhere he'd never make it out and end up out of gas on Indian Paint Brush Drive.

I tell him how I drove all up and down the franchise strip, past Taco Cabaña, Jack in the Box, the Four Seasons: Mustard, Mayo, Catsup, A-1. And that he has no idea how many red cars there are in San Antonio, cruising down the middle of the street, or on a side street nosing into traffic, or jumping a yellow light at an intersection. Maybe a million I say.

I'm in my sheet, with the hand against my cheek, trying to calm down and get myself into a frame of mind to pose.

Henry has taken my hair out of its braid, because he's not in the mood for the Indian now, and he's brushing it out while I tell him about Dad showing up at Glenna's.

"If I'd been along that wouldn't have happened," he says.

"What? Dad?"

"Your running away."

How does he know that?

"If I'd been with you, what would you have done when he showed up?"

"I don't know."

"You would have said, 'There's Dad.' "

"Yes." I can see that what he says is true. I'd have seen that car and frozen and grabbed Henry's sleeve, and then told him, "That's Dad." And then waited. Because Henry would have known what to do.

So how come he knows that, I'm wondering. And how come that's true?

"What would I have done?"

"I don't know."

"Gone over and shook his hand and asked him how was the drilling business going." Henry says it "bidness" and that makes me giggle a little, his putting on that accent. "What would your dad have done?"

"He'd have told you that hair oil costs more than crude and that the only thing people are interested in putting in a hole these days—" And then I really do giggle. "Saying, 'Pardon me, ladies,' to Glenna and me, if we were around."

I know what Henry is trying to tell me, that I have to deal with who they are right now. That at Brogan's phone customers' party I should have introduced Dad to a couple of clients who were big on diamond bits or whatever they're using these days. That I should have taken a glass of wine off Mom-the-waiter's tray and said, Thanks I sure do need this, my whistle's dry, and then gone right back to talking to the women ranchers.

Is that right?

I can see it sounds right when he says it, see it clear as day, but what Henry doesn't understand is that something can be right and you can't do it. Because you've spent all your life *not* doing it, so you can't suddenly say that you were wrong to have a fear of heights and so trot out on a high wire, or fear of falling and go jump out of an airplane. Some ways of acting get set in you when you're young because they're all you know how to do, and then they stay with you, like stuttering or left-handedness.

"You don't understand," I tell him.

"Let's talk about this running away," he says.

"I tried to do what you said, but I couldn't. Just sit there."

I'm thinking that it's easy for Henry to say that my folks won't do anything if I don't pay any attention to them, but that only means he doesn't know them. He's thinking of his polite Mrs. Kraft-Wozencrantz with her formal-informal dinners. He's not thinking of Midge Temple and Turk Jackson, grown people, pulling some kid back and forth like a couple of hounds with a rubber chicken. He's thinking of himself, Henry, a boy who could go back and find his daddy and then go hang around his uncle, because if he didn't show up nobody was going to come looking for him, and if they didn't look up and see him, nobody was going to wonder where he was.

"You ran off and left your actor friend at your aunt and uncle's party."

"I thought you didn't want me to see L.W."

"We're not talking about the matter of this boy in your life when I need you to concentrate on what we're doing because the show is only two weeks away. We're talking about your running away."

Sometimes the way Henry says things reminds me of Mom. I halfway expect to hear him say, Are you listening, Jolene?

"Do you hear what I'm saying?"

"You sound like Mom." I have to laugh.

"All the better. She seems able to get your undivided attention on any and every occasion."

I move my head so he can't touch my hair.

He's sorry and says, I'm sorry, a couple of times. He says let's sit at the table and have a cup of cocoa. I think he's going to want to make love again, but he's already moved on from that.

He takes my hand, my real hand, and then he lays his uncle's mistress's hand on top of our hands. And his other hand on top of that.

"About running away," he says.

"I can't help it. I had too many years of running away with Dad or running away with Mom, and now whenever I see them I guess my legs just start to go. Anyway, at least I didn't leave town with her after Brogan's party and end up someplace where you could never find me, in some 'burb so big you'd still be looking for me when your show is over. And I didn't go off with him today, head out for some rented house where he still probably thinks he can leave me with a sitter eating Rocky Road ice cream."

"I want you to make me a promise."

"I don't like to do that."

"When was the last time you made a promise?"

"They were always after me to promise—"

"Jolene."

"What?"

"Will you forget your mom and dad?" He says this and his voice sounds back to being mad again, but then he buries his face for a minute in the pile of hands and I don't know for sure where he is.

"You asked me when was the last time—"

"I want you to make me a promise."

"I don't like to do that."

"It's a promise you won't want to keep."

"Then why am I going to make it?"

"Because. Because a long time from now you'll be glad you did."

"Tell me what it is." I think he means something about running away from Mom and Dad, or maybe about not going to see L.W., and there doesn't seem to be any point in saying I'm not going to do what I'm going to do.

"Promise me that you will not run away after the Fine Arts show."

"But I won't be posing any more, will I?"

"I'm not talking about your running off from the studio; I'm talking about your running away from the museum. I'm asking you to promise that you will not run away from the show."

I think about going with him to the little museum with the red, brown, blue, and white blankets, and remember that he knew how to make me feel safe, even when his mother showed up. And I think about the Western Artifacts show when we got the antler mirror, and I was being a dealer, and we had a good time.

But then I remember that those other times were different: they were before Mom and Dad had crashed the scene. What if the chaps-and-spurs dealer had turned out not to be a dealer after all, and had waved four fingers at me? What if the curator of the little museum had been Dad in another, wavier hairpiece? What would I have done? I look at Henry and I know I can trust him, but I'm not so sure about me. I don't want to make him a promise I can't keep, so I pull my hand, my bottom hand, from the stack. "Do you mean if one of them—?"

"Forget Mom and Dad." This time he actually shouts at me.

I mess with the sheet.

He warms up our cocoa. "Promise me," he says, calm again and through with being upset.

I think about it, about how if Henry is with me then it will be different. About how this matters a lot to him. "Okay," I say.

"This will require a blood oath."

"Henry!"

He gets out the box of hands, and something from another drawer that looks like a pot of lip gloss, but must be paint, because he wets his finger in his mouth and dips it in the pot, and paints a red drop on both my hands and his hands, in the same place on the inside of the wrist, and then on a couple of my favorite of the uncle's woman's hands, an early porcelain one, a metal one in its fleshy sleeve. Then he presses all our wrists together.

"I, Jolene, do promise Henry . . ."

I'm getting the giggles again. "I, Jolene, do promise Henry."

"Not to run away at our show."

"Not to run away at our show."

"On my oath."

"On my oath."

"So help me."

"So—help me." I hide my mouth.

He puts the paint and hands away, all but the one I'm going to use. He wipes the paint, which is soft, like lipstick, off our wrists.

Then, holding mine circled in his fingers, he says real low, "I don't want to hurt you."

"You?"

"They'll say odalisque. Matisse. They'll say Matisse. The press have meager minds. They lack talent. The only thing they can draw is comparisons. Maybe I should hang a couple of my uncle's. Let them compare Wozencrantz with Wozencrantz. That's the thing to do."

"I don't understand."

"You will," he says, pulling off the sheet and leading me in to pose.

32

"IS IT FAR?" Cissy whines. She is not enthusiastic about this family outing. She's dressed in an aqua pantsuit, nothing fancy, not her good-luck clothes that she saves for bingo. Her hair is a kind of dyed red that Glenna calls henna and Mom calls drugstore red. She has what Mom also calls a maximum fidget factor, which is why she's so tiny no matter what she eats, and that isn't much anyway, because she goes crazy sitting still at a dinner table.

"Nothing's far in San Antonio," Brogan tells her. "San Antonio—our part of it I'm talking about here—is just one little slice of pecan pie. You've got Loop 410 is the crust, and then right down cutting through all the pecans and sweet part you've got Broadway and New Braunfels, with the tip just nudging Fort Sam. If it's not inside the loop; if it's not off Broadway or New Braunfels, then it's not in what's your true city of San Antonio."

"What about San Pedro?" I ask him, thinking of L.W.'s house on Rosewood, which is halfway between where he goes to school at Trinity and where I used to go, at San Antonio College. That's right at the heart of the city, it seems to me, closer to downtown, and makes a wedge of its own with the Fine Arts Museum at the end.

"*San* what?" Brogan says and laughs. "Must be some other town, *San Whatever;* that's not a piece of the pie I was referring to. That's some other piece of pie, maybe your coconut or your banana icebox, but that's not your pecan pie, if you get my meaning."

I do, even if I don't agree with him. But maybe that's why L.W.'s house feels so safe to me: Brogan doesn't even know where that part of the city is.

"If you say so," Cissy says. "But beats me what we're all dressed up to go see."

"We are going to view this architectural marvel of the twentieth century designed by your former New York City architect, which, according to my newspaper here, has a palm house one hundred and ten feet in diameter and fifty-five feet tall—your basic giant erector set—that is going to be filled with palm trees, and which also has a reflecting pool, a sunken fern room, a spiral terrace, and your big arcade for promenading with a Platonic tree in the middle. Now if this—and I'm quoting here, I'm quoting from my newspaper—if this greenhouse, this Fern Barn, in which 'plants are not merely nurtured but brought into a vibrant architectural dialogue' is exactly ten minutes from this very house where we're sitting on the patio having our morning pineapple juice, then I say we're wasting the six million dollars it cost and it's our civic duty to climb into the Oldsmobile and go see it for ourselves."

"Six billion dollars?" Glenna gets out her ballpoint and begins to calculate. "That's four million MasterCards, figure a fifteen-hundred-dollar limit a card, that's four MasterCards each for every man, woman, and child, legal and illegal, in the city of San Antonio."

"Million." Hoyt sets her straight. "Six million."

"Wait a minute then." She recalculates. "Why, that's different. Imagine, that's only four thousand MasterCards total. Figure four people, average, a household, to make it come out even, why if just one out of every two hundred and fifty families donated just one MasterCard each they could pay for the whole thing."

"Some bigwig donated the money. Named it for his wife or something. A philanthropist shelled out the capital, Glenna."

"I was just saying what if they were having to raise the money, that's what I was saying. You have to get some idea what it means, translate it down where people can figure it out. I mean what does six billion mean to people? Nothing. It's a number, that's what."

"Six million."

"That's what I'm saying. I'm saying six *billion* is four MasterCards apiece for every living soul in the city and six *million* is one MasterCard for every two hundred and fifty people. Now most folks don't know that; they don't know the difference. They throw those numbers around. I mean, for example, if the federal budget or the weapon wars were translated into something your average person could understand, that would keep us out of debt. The President could say to the people: 'Now this nuclear device is going to cost every citizen and alien in the USA exactly six MasterCards each. Is that okay with you? Are you game?' And the chances are that people would say, 'Are you kidding?' "

Cissy is still fidgeting. She hasn't got the point yet of what this big excursion is about. Normally, she and Hoyt like to spend their Sundays waiting for Mondays, on account of they can't gamble on Sundays.

"I didn't get my beauty sleep," Cissy complains.

"Why didn't you get your beauty sleep?" Brogan asks.

"Because the charcoal-briquet lobby moved daylight saving from the end of the month where it belongs to the first of the month where it doesn't."

"You didn't get your beauty sleep because you bought a dozen extra bingo cards last night."

"Four."

I'm slightly nervous, going out in public. But Henry is hanging the show and said it was bad luck for me to watch. He says, anyway, that I have to practice being out in public so I won't be jumpy at the opening next week. That the Botanical Gardens sounds like a great idea: the grounds will be wall-to-wall people, who I'll have to push my way through. Sunday gardeners most of them, coming for the official opening of the palm house and the fern room.

He gave me a kiss when he walked me to my car, which was something different on his part. Usually when I left—or at least how it was before I moved in with him—he'd open the door the way you do for a cat who's scratching to go outside and let it out and then go back about your business until you hear it scratching to get back in again.

"See here." Brogan shows his mother the story in the paper. "They've got a lot of native areas, see—that's the old part of the gardens—that show different parts of the state, the Hill Country, South Texas, which is us. See, it says mesquite, huisache, retama, cacti, sotol, yucca. You girls can take a look, settle your argument about which tree is which tree."

"Huisache is the one with the green bark. I don't have to put on hose and a girdle to know that," Cissy says.

"That's retama," Glenna tells her, "that has the green bark. You get them mixed up. They both have yellow flowers so you get them mixed up."

"I guess I do not get them mixed up," Cissy says, "as I happen to have a tree with a green bark growing in my very own yard next to the sweet gum; I just happen to have a native huisache plain as day in my own yard located on Lot 4, Block 48, aka 123 Savoy, which just happens to belong to me."

"You yourself and no one else?" Hoyt asks her.

"You and me. That's me. This is a community property state, don't forget. You and me equals me in this state."

"That's a retama in your yard," Glenna says.

Hoyt has been doing some figuring of his own. He is wearing boots, faded jeans, a leather belt with a big silver buckle with a raised longhorn on it, white shirt, and a real bomber jacket from the Second World War, he claims, although Brogan says his dad didn't fly any missions, being only a supply sergeant in the States for the whole time. Now Brogan asks Hoyt did he know the outfit he has on some yuppie is right this very week paying $900 for, and Hoyt says that that yuppie is getting took.

"What I'm trying to figure here," Hoyt says, "is what would be the mortgage on a place like that." He has a white mustache but his thick hairpiece is coal black. "You figure you got the palm home, the fern pit, the whatyoucallit with the tree, the walkway—you can't figure the price of that like you can a basic three-two plus or minus school district and extras. But, okay, six million. Figure it straight. The bank has said six million, you check your Fanny Maes, you check your adjustable rates, so ten percent down, that leaves you five mil four. Okay, if, say, a mortgage of sixty thou runs you six hundred a month, P-I-T-I, then that'd be, on the Fern Barn, that'd be a monthly payment of fifty-four thousand. That's a whale of a lot of interest deduction for your benefactor; that's not just a philanthropic itch you've got here."

Glenna frowns, then takes her finger and smooths the lines away. "I don't think that's the way they do it, Daddy Temple. I think they give the full amount, donors like that."

"You think they shell out six million in cash and tell the IRS and the IRS says, Fine, Big Donor, take that sum right off the top of your taxes? Not likely. It's spread out. Has got to be."

"What it is," Brogan says, "is your typical Texas venture. Every second person in the state is filing a Chapter Eleven, real estate has bottomed out, snake oil is going for more than crude, and San Antonio is showing little d that we can spend six million dollars on culture. That's what's going on."

"I guess I know what's in my own backyard," Cissy says. "I guess I know a huisache when I see it every day of my life."

. . .

The Botanical Gardens are actually about twenty years old, and mostly are an outdoor museum with different spots that try to look like different areas of the state, and in the paper it showed all these new buildings rising up out of big dirt mounds behind the old part. But when we turn into the grounds of the gardens (right before the entrance to Fort Sam), all we see is a whole lot of other cars. It's really crowded, not just because of the opening but also because the weather has not yet turned to baking hot and people are in the mood to get out and take a good look at each other before they spend four months huddled around their air conditioners. They want to be sure that other people are still alive and kicking, doing their civic Sunday thing, and haven't crawled off like sick dogs in some corner, because of their puny bank balances or unsettling investments.

In the gatehouse there is a poster about a talk on the South Central Texas Xeriscape, "The Conservation of Water Through Creative Landscaping," and another for a lecture on "Papaya Trees: Culture and Hybridization."

Right away, Cissy has a fit about the ticket. "When's the drawing?" she asks the woman standing behind the desk.

"Drawing?" the woman repeats. She's selling tickets and hoping to sell some booklets about the local flora as well. She's in the sort of rose-colored dress with matching jacket that makes me think she's probably a volunteer, giving up her Sunday afternoon to help out this cultural cause.

"The *drawing*," Cissy says.

"There is no drawing."

"Well, there's no number on this ticket. You want us to write our names on the back? You need a name for a door prize if you don't have a number."

"It's just an admission ticket, ma'am."

"No door prize? You mean we pay a dollar fifty for *nothing*? We *give* you one dollar and fifty cents? That doesn't entitle us to a chance on anything?"

"Come on." Brogan takes her arm. "Let the folks in line behind us get in."

"Can you believe it?" Cissy whines. "No door prize."

"We could all chip in a dollar," Hoyt says. "There's five of us, make that two dollars, have ourselves a private drawing. Ten dollars—"

"Come on, come on."

"It's a rip-off, if you ask me," Cissy mutters as Glenna takes charge and leads us through the doorway of the gatehouse out into a lovely planted area with a vine-covered archway to one side and a Lone Star–shaped fountain in front of us. Up ahead, naturally, we expect to see the main attraction:

the fifty-five-foot-tall palm house filled with, I guess, palm trees. But we don't.

A lot of other people are looking around, too.

People who don't seem like they come from Brogan's slice of the pie. There are a couple of Indian women in saris with smudges on their foreheads; some woman pushing another one in a wheelchair; some very short Mexican nuns in heavy black robes and white hats like you don't see much any more. There is a frizzy-haired blind lady, who is doing a lot of smelling, and I wonder if they didn't let her dog come in with her, but she seems to be managing with a cane. The only men are part of couples, usually white-haired ladies in also pastel volunteer-looking Sunday dresses with jackets, and men in stiff white shirts and black string ties, weathered as ranchers, looking around trying to decide how come they are at this place and if they know anybody they see.

While I am busy trying not to jump out of my skin thinking that every single one of them, no matter what the size or shape or shade or sex, is either Midge Temple (knees bent, playing a short Mexican nun? eyes blank, playing a frizzy-haired blind lady? foreign-speaking, playing an Indian in muted red with oiled black hair?) or Turk Jackson (in elevator shoes, in a gray toupee, in heavy suntan pancake makeup, playing a onetime football player, an old Texas settler, a West Texas rancher). In fact, I can hardly walk along with Brogan and Glenna and Hoyt and Cissy—four-square protection— without getting the total jumpy creeps.

We, along with most of the crowd, look here and there, behind us and to each side, trying to spot the main, newspaper-promised attraction.

Most people have their 35-millimeters out and are taking shots: of each other, of special plants, such as the bulging green oblongs hanging from a fan-shaped bush, of the star-shaped fountain.

"Where's the Fern Barn?" Brogan asks in a loud voice.

"Don't ask me," somebody answers him.

"Your guess is as good as mine," says another.

What's clear to everyone is that what's going on is construction. Up ahead on a high rise is an old summerhouse with an iron rooster on top. Close ahead, past the planted areas, we can see a fence, and on the other side of that all over the rolling little mounds, semi-hills, workers in hard hats, surveyors, pieces of metal tubing and frames in the process of being assembled.

We crowd as close as is possible to the fence, and are able to spot a big hole covered over with some plastic stuff, that Brogan decides must be going to be the sunken fern garden. The palm cone has about one bottom bunch of metal pieces on one side. There is a large scooped-out place, big as a shopping mall almost, that must be going to be the arcade and the reflecting pool. This opening is clearly not the real opening; there will be an official one next year, with the big donor cutting some ribbons and pictures in the paper—the same pictures we already saw in Brogan's paper, which must have been of the architect's models.

"You know what we're seeing?" Hoyt asks.

"I know what we're seeing," Brogan says. "Some construction workers working time-and-a-half for overtime."

"We're seeing some future oil field. You and me are standing on the site of a future South Texas field."

"How's that?"

Hoyt adjusts his silver belt buckle with a thumb. "You know what oil is? Oil is ferns plus a few billion years. Right? Well, what if the oil fields we got now were some Neanderthal's former Fern Barn?

"What if they were a showy greenhouse that he opened up for the other Neanderthals to see? Price: a piece of fresh meat. He showed it off, his sunken fern room, his palm house, the whole bit, and then after a time it all packed down under somebody else's feet—latecomers, us after a while—and then by that time it had been squooshed until it had turned to black slime and then black crude and then the latecomers, us, piped it out.

"Well, same here. We're gazing at some future well site. Gives you a thrill, boy, to look at it that way, doesn't it?"

Hearing how everybody is busy not seeing what they see makes me think about Henry's show and have some sympathy for him. What if it will be the same at his opening? A bunch of people showing up and wandering around because they read in the paper that this local artist was showing off his giant mountains and bridges (shoulders and knees, but they wouldn't know that), and some of them are hoping for door prizes or drawings and some of them are looking for dates, but none of them see the pictures. And after they wander around a while, they decide to all go to Lou Tess and eat, because they're all dressed up anyway, and then call it an afternoon.

It makes me sad for people who work so hard to try to do something special, and, on impulse, I give Glenna a big hug. She doesn't understand, but likes it and whispers to me, "So you're happy where you are, aren't you, hon?"

We wander back under the archway, which Brogan says is a big grapevine, and then he calls to us, "Here, girls, here's your native trees."

Cissy and Glenna drag their heels while I walk over to where he's standing in front of a replica of an old-time rancher's house. We read the sign that says:

ADOBE STRUCTURE with vertical cedar posts, chinking and plastering.

"Here, over here," he calls out. "Right here are the native trees."

We can see a little grove of South Texas vegetation, but

Glenna and Cissy don't want to look too close, because they can see that everything is labeled in plain English, and so one of them stands to be the loser of their argument.

I say I'll do the reading for them, so they won't have to put their glasses on, and I've decided ahead of time to leave out any mention of bark color, but I don't need to worry, because the Botanical people haven't mentioned it either.

With the women nervous as cats, I read aloud:

SCREW BEAN: Mimosa family, height to twenty-five feet, yellow flowers, thorny, beans used for syrup.
RETAMA: Senna family, height to twenty-five feet, yellow flowers, needlelike leaves with medicinal properties.
HUISACHE: Mimosa family, height to twenty-five feet, yellow flowers, fernlike leaves, good honey plant.

"If you ask me," Cissy remarks, relieved, "there's not a hill of beans difference between any of them."

"I have to agree," Glenna says. "I think everything we're seeing here is mesquite. I think they planted a bunch of mesquite, one person did that, and then another person came along and copied stuff from her garden book."

"Not a one of them looks like what's in my yard at Lot 4, Block 48, aka 123 Savoy, that's for sure."

"How can we tell anyway? None of them is in bloom."

We head back to the deep shady archway to pose for Glenna's camera.

People keep getting in the way, the lady in the wheelchair, the blind lady with her cane, one of the Indian women, a nun crossing herself, but that makes it a public place, having the corner of somebody else in the picture, and some of the white-haired ladies married to the men in string ties take pictures, too, and there isn't a lot of grumbling about the fact that we've all come out to see something that isn't there. Because we've got photos to show for it anyway.

Brogan says it seems like everybody understands that the bottom has dropped out of things and that San Antone has rallied and built itself a cultural event that's competitive with the best, and that's the main thing. Everybody used to say Remember the Alamo, like we'd done something wonderful to all get killed; now they were going to be saying Remember the Fern Barn. Remember the time we sunk six million into some metal rods and piles of dirt and showed little d what High Art was all about, when we didn't any of us have much more than the price of the ticket to get in the door.

Brogan likes this idea that he's developed, and he shouts out real loud, to laughter from all the people standing nearby: "Remember the Fern Barn!"

So Hoyt gets into the mood of it, and, with the toe of his boot, draws a line in the dirt, which Brogan steps across, dragging an imaginary wounded leg, and all the time Glenna is getting this on film.

Then, as if on cue, Mom, looking just like Mom, in her piano-teacher blue, with her home-perm hair, pushes through the crowd, steps over the line, and falls in a heap at her brother's feet.

"What in the world?" Hoyt looks down.

"Mom." Being next of kin, I make the identification.

"Midge?" Glenna bends over her, making sure.

We are all now in a half-circle, our backs turned to the curious bystanders who think maybe someone has had a heat stroke, but it isn't that hot, or maybe had a heart attack, but, no, it's a woman.

I look all around me at the landscape with its copies of other landscapes dotted on it, but my feet don't make a move, because this scene has a familiar quality to it: fishy. It's like Dad said at Brogan's, Some things don't change, and one of them is Mom, who is definitely not one to commit an accident. She's never fainted in her life and would die before she'd do it with a hundred nosy-parker people looking on. Therefore, she must be up to her old tricks again. Proving that the best way to be invisible is to be conspicuous.

"She's white as a sheet," Glenna frets.

"Her eyes have rolled back in her head." Brogan stares at his sister in a panic.

Cissy squats down in her aqua pantsuit and pulls up Mom's eyelids, checking for herself. "Maybe it's a convulsion." She tries out that idea.

"Looks like shock to me," Hoyt pronounces.

"I think it's walking pneumonia," Glenna decides. "Listen to her breathe; her lungs have filled up."

"She's not walking so how can it be walking pneumonia?" Cissy argues.

"It's a figure of speech."

Brogan stands up and makes the decision, being the one responsible. "We'll have to take her to the Emergency."

But this bothers him, because there are no hospitals in his piece of the pie and you can tell he's racking his brain to think of where is the nearest place to turn his sister over to someone who knows what's going on, to get her off his hands. But Hoyt and Cissy have Medicare and they know all the ins and outs. After a few minutes' delay in which they argue over whether to make it Baptist Memorial or Humana Metropolitan, they pick the latter and soon Brogan is carrying Mom's all-but-lifeless body out of the Botanical Gardens' Xeriscape into his Olds.

He puts her in the back seat with me, her head in my lap, while he follows Hoyt's lead through the city's empty Sunday streets, into my part of town.

"Are you sure she's breathing?" Glenna asks me, frantic in the front seat.

"She's okay," I report, bending my head close to Mom's face.

"How'm I doing?" Mom whispers.

"Never better," I whisper back.

"I need a rest," she says in my ear, giving a loud, pitiful wheeze for the benefit of eavesdroppers. "Spring me in a week."

33

ONE OF MOM'S RULES was that every move should provide an education.

"Before we're through," she liked to say, "you'll be a master of the geography of the state. You'll have the flora and the fauna in the palm of your hand."

Everywhere we went, we did field trips to all the points of interest around our temporary homes, those near our suburbs. We saw the Big Thicket from Beauregard Heights, Lake Wright Patman from Honey Grove Hills, Guadalupe Peak from Pass-of-the-Camels Park, Palo Duro Canyon from Tierra Blanca Estates, the Aransas Wildlife Preserve from Espiritu Santo Shores, but first of all, at the start of it all, we saw the Bracken Cave of Bats, from Devil's River Bluffs.

This was back before Mom had hit on the idea of giving piano lessons, back before she learned that Dad had the get-up-and-go to track us anywhere, back when cash was tight and whatever car we had was usually good for one round trip before it went back to the shop.

It was when she first got the idea of picking up postcards

from a bunch of little towns to send to Dad and Brogan, so we'd bought stacks from places like Baby Head, Hog Wallow, Tan Tought, Dead Man, Oat Meal, Fly Gap, circling around our final destination: our first 'burb. Really more exurb than suburb, it was a bare half hour from the San Antonio city limits.

Mom said she didn't want to go any farther down what she called the backside of Texas, where there was nothing between you and the Mexican border but wild horses, rattlers, vinegarones, renegade Indians, and flash-flooded creek beds.

The night I'm remembering was back before the escape from the airport with me in the wig, back when I was just a little kid, not yet in school, back when Mom and Dad were doing a warm-up to the idea of stealing me back and forth, when they were young and new to the game. Right after the white handkerchief phase.

Mom told me after supper, the first night in our rented house, "Get your sweater, we're going out. It might get cool. This country around here on the backside runs hot and cold; hot in the day and cold at night. You have to stay prepared. And wear socks. Haven't you got socks? I bought you socks. No telling what's crawling around in the brush out in the country. Ticks and tarantulas and who knows what. This is the *country* where we're going, this is not your civilization. This is not your nice safe city out here."

We drove away from Devil's River Bluffs across a sort of purple hilly landscape, parked and sat outside on a bunch of rocks with maybe a hundred other people. I didn't know what we were doing, but suddenly the sun slipped down and it was twilight and then what looked like a huge column of black smoke began to pour out of the open mouth of the cave in front of us and rise into the sky.

Bats.

Mom said we only sat there two hours; she said that sometimes it took four hours for all the bats just to fly out, there were that many of them. That they were all mommies, one million of them plus, each of them looking to eat her weight in moths for supper. She said that every single mother bat had a pink baby bat hanging by its heels from the ceiling of that cave, so that there were a million plus babies in there, all hanging upside down, looking like unborn baby puppies, and that each mommy could tell her kid from all the rest.

She said that after the one million bat mothers had eaten about a hundred and fifty tons of moths they would all come swarming back into the big old cave and each one would zoom right to her very own particular baby bat, hanging upside down waiting for her. And wasn't that amazing, that she could find her own in a crowd that size?

"You can't even imagine, Jolene, how many unborn-puppy baby bats that would be, and each one being found just like that"—she snapped her fingers—"by her mom. That's called *radar*. That's what a mom has," she said, "that no one else has got. Are you listening? I'm trying to educate you. I'm trying to educate you to the basic wonders of the natural world. What a mom has where her own kid is concerned is, don't you forget it, full-fledged radar."

34

*H*ENRY IS MORE NERVOUS than I am before the show.

He spends a lot of time getting us dressed. He's in a tuxedo, but then he says that what he's wearing is tails. And turns so I can see the tails and then explains about the white tie. I ask him why, because you expect to see an artist dressed the way I saw him at the opening at the Sun Dog the night I first met him, in that faded work shirt the same way that the other painter, whose face I don't remember any more, was dressed.

He says there are a lot of reasons. First, because everybody will not be expecting it. Second, because his mother wants him to dress up. Third, because there will be media scrounging around wanting shots. Fourth—and when I hear this I know it is the real reason and the rest of what he's saying is just cover—his uncle wore tails the first time he had a show of his mistress with the hand, in her cape. Henry is being his uncle for the evening, and I can understand that. It's sort of a costume. And with his mother there, and maybe his daughter, he'll need a costume.

I haven't told Brogan and Glenna about the show. I just went to an opening with them—and Hoyt and Cissy and, it turned out, Mom—and that's enough public stuff with the Temple family for a while. Anyway, I didn't think I could handle that, having them there, when I was concentrating on doing what Henry wants me to, and being around a crowd of people. Besides, this is Henry's show. Except for his mother nobody will know me, and I am semi-used to her by now and how she is with me, treating me like somebody she is supposed to notice but not really noticing me.

He wants me to wear a long black dress, real plain, with no sleeves and a round neck, and I try it on and it fits just right. After he mentions his uncle, I have the idea of what we're doing, and ask him right out if he wants me to wear the velvet cape that his uncle's woman wore.

He does, and he's already fixed it up, with a hand fastened inside the lining (by its skinlike glove) so that when I have it on, you can just see the tips of the fingers sticking out.

He messes with my hair until he gets impatient with himself and looks at the clock. It isn't what he wants. First he braids it and then he brushes it back out. He's made up my face—painted it, I guess you could say—making my brows heavier and my mouth redder, which fits the black outfit.

Finally, I figure out what I need to do. I ask him to let me see one of the photographs of his uncle's woman.

He hesitates, stalls around, says he hasn't got time to hunt one up, but I know he knows where they are.

After a few minutes, he gets out a box from a closet behind some of his paints in the studio, and hands me two. I am amazed, I have to admit, because she does look like me. She looks more like me than I do, if that makes sense. I get over that as fast as I can, because I want to help him out. So I study her, how she looks, and I study the effect until I feel like I'm the person in the pictures, and then I turn to Henry and don't say anything but I lift my head way up like it was pulled by a string, and then drop my shoulders and push them way back, as if they were trying to touch.

He looks very pleased and tells me that I've got it. Then, while I'm holding myself that way, which feels quite different and strong, he powders my neck with white powder, so, I know, it looks even longer than it does because of the way I'm standing.

He looks back and forth from me to the picture and then he dusts some of the white powder on the sides of my nose, too. And then he is very happy. He kisses my eyelids and my paler nose and my longer neck, and I can feel him being really happy and pleased with everything.

That makes me not as nervous, because if Henry is happy that way, if he's fixed us up the way he wants to, then he can carry the evening off and it won't be anything to worry about.

He gives me a beauty mark on my cheek and then takes it off. He is still fussing around, although it's time for us to go. He looks at the photograph and then at me again.

I see that the mistress's cape has a wide bow that ties it in the front, but that this one, which is either another one or the old one that's been changed, fastens with a clasp. I tell him to go get a black ribbon, which he does, and then I have him tie it around my neck, and he likes that.

Just when we're about to leave he takes a white orchid out of a box and pins it on my shoulder, so that we both are dressed in black and white. And all of a sudden I feel excited, as if I had a date to a costume party and didn't have anything to worry about and was going to have a lot of fun.

35

THE FINE ARTS is in the old Lone Star Brewery, the kind of unused building cities usually tear down, but the kind that lately Texans are anxious to save to show that they are being historical and cultural. Or that's what Brogan would say.

It is yellow brick, the old faded kind, with curved brick arches over large windows on every wall. It has two towers that are four stories high, and in the middle a two-story part that's the entrance now. High in the air, like a circus tightrope, is a glass walkway connecting one tower with another.

The sidewalk and yard around it are also all paved with brick and there are big welded sculptures that must be bolted to the ground so no one will steal them. Some of the windows on the back, I see, have bars, and Henry says that's so no one can climb in and steal the museum's prize collection, which is a lot of valuable Near Eastern bronzes and ceramics. He says that Fine Arts also owns some paintings by artists who are favorites of his—Segal, Schonzeit, Pearlstein—but that we won't be looking at them today. Today we'll be looking at his work only.

We go in the back door, past a guard, and I see that all the signs are bilingual (IN THE MUSEUM / EN EL MUSEO . . . LOOK, ENJOY / MIRAR, DISFRUTAR . . .) and that reminds me of L.W. I wonder if I should have told him and Archie about the show, but am glad I didn't. The way Henry and I are together right now, I don't think that would be a good way to be with L.W. around. Besides, this is Henry's show and I don't think he ought to have to wonder what's going on with me and anybody else.

Mostly, I guess I didn't tell them because I can't do but one thing at a time, and right now what I'm doing is being with Henry.

As soon as we step in the door, someone screams, "There he is." And someone else calls, "Look, back there," and then all the people, maybe a hundred, who are waiting at the front door turn around and rush at Henry.

"Who are they?" I ask him, freezing for a minute, then remembering and raising my head and pushing my shoulders back, making my throat look long.

"It's a little pre-show party," he says. "Mother's doing."

Mrs. Wozencrantz comes over to us, and the women I met at the Navajo show. She says their names again and reminds Henry that Hallie is the Friends of the Fine Arts and Millie is Friends of the little museum, the Bernais. That the two of them have got their groups to put on a reception for Henry before the official opening, to which anybody can come, begins. It's a private party, in other words, by invitation, although I see a lot of cameras everywhere.

The women, and mostly they are women, are all dressed up in the kind of dress that goes with six strands of pearls—

expensive, heavy, and to the floor. There is a scattering of men, a couple in tails like Henry, most of them in suits, and even one in a black cape like mine who raises his brows at me in a friendly way and nods his head.

They stand in clusters, the friends, staring at Henry, who doesn't seem to mind it. I hear my name a couple of times, carried across the stone floor in a loud whisper, Jolene, isn't that, doesn't she, Jolene, and that makes me get a really tight feeling and my hands begin to sweat. But then I remember about looking like the uncle's woman and that I promised Henry I wouldn't run away, and I calm down.

At one point Mrs. Wozencrantz takes me to one side for a few minutes. She is talking to me in a low voice, leaning her head in very close until I can smell her breath which smells like perfume. She's so close that I can even see thin gold crowns on her back teeth and hear the sort of click her tongue makes against her front teeth. "Henry has made your fortune, my dear, you do know that, don't you? He's made your fortune as well as his own with this show."

"Thank you," I answer, not knowing what else to say.

I don't know if she wants to know how things are with me and Henry, and I wouldn't know what to tell her if she did. I don't think she wants him to have anyone closer to him than she is, and I imagine she didn't like his wives at all, but I'm not sure I'm any closer to him than they were. We're not measurable that way. I just pose and he paints and sometimes we are doing it or other things that connect to the painting. But that's not something you can put into words. Anyway, not to somebody like Mrs. Wozencrantz, who is going around being the Artist's Mother, and that's not anything that anybody can get closer than because that's something in her mind that shuts out anybody real, even Henry.

In a minute he sees that I am with his mother and comes over to adjust my cape and touch my hair, the way he does when he's about to start painting, and it reminds me about posing, that that's what I'm doing now, and as soon as he smooths the hair behind my ear and runs his hand along my neck where the white powder is, I relax.

One other time I get cornered during the reception. It's almost at the end, when a few of the people waiting outside, the general public, are peering through the locked front doors, trying to see what's going on, and some are even tapping on the heavy glass. It's when Henry's daughter comes walking up to me.

She looks the same as she did when I met her, like she'd be more at home with dogs and horses, with her deep suntan and her light eyelashes and hair. She's wearing a short pink dress and her legs are long and dark brown.

"Hi," she says. "Remember me?"

"You're Karen."

"You aren't an antique dealer. I knew it. I knew you were lying."

"I'm a model. But your grandmother knew that all along, didn't she?"

"I did, too," she says, but I don't believe her.

I lift my cape and show her the hand attached.

"Yuck," she says.

"Your daddy pretends that I'm the woman his uncle used to photograph. I look like her. I wonder if your mother did, too."

"Do I?"

I walk all around Karen, pretending to take my time studying her. "No," I say, finally. "She had coarser features. She was not really pretty the way you are. She had this dark coloring and big features and so she photographed well."

"Did Dad dream up that outfit for you?"

"Yes."

"It looks like a costume."

She slips away toward her grandmother, then comes back. "Thanks," she says. "That was nice about looking pretty. You don't lie worth a damn, but that was nice." She grabs the artificial hand and gives it a shake and we both laugh.

Henry has me come and pose for some pictures. In a couple of them we are facing each other, which I don't like a lot because I'm not confident about my profile. In a couple more we are looking straight out at the camera and he tells me not to smile, so I don't. In one he has me reach down and hold the hand up to my chest. I curve my own hand around it, and that brings a blush to my face that I can feel, hot all over my cheeks, because it reminds me of what I've got on when I pose. But Henry is standing near me and he says, Don't smile, chin up, look at the camera, hold the hand higher, the sort of instructions that he gives me when we're in the studio alone and I follow the sound of his voice the way I do when he's painting, and that has the effect of making all the friends of the two museums fade away, the way you see in films when everything gets blurred. Then I'm not nervous any more, but just listening to Henry.

"What name shall we use?" one of the people with a camera asks him.

"Jolene," he says and spells it.

"Last name?"

"No last name. Just Jolene."

I turn to him, touched that he is remembering about Mom and Dad and not getting the Temple or Jackson in there, and not getting it in there for Brogan and Glenna either.

I eat a cookie and have some punch that doesn't have alcohol in it and then a cup of some that must have wine; then Henry comes over and wipes my mouth with his handkerchief and walks me toward a set of stairs that is roped off but that leads to a second floor Mexican Folk Art show. While he's patting my face I look up overhead and think about the glass skywalk, and just for a minute I wish I were up there and not down here, but then I get over that.

"Remember what you promised," Henry says.

I nod. "I didn't run away when Mom turned up, needing a rest, at the Fern Barn," I remind him. "Not even when I had to help make it stick, getting her admitted to Emergency."

"No matter what."

"I already said I wouldn't."

"Hear what I'm saying."

"I do," I tell him, thinking that we've been over this about a dozen times already.

"In the beginning I wanted the paintings. Now I want you, too. I don't want to lose you. Will you remember that?"

"Yes."

"Because I love you, and this is all I have to give you. Do you understand?"

"I don't know." He says it so seriously, that he loves me. Like he was about to get killed in a war or go back to some wife or die of an awful cancer, one of those times in films when you know that it's going to be over, because if it wasn't going to be over then he wouldn't be telling her that he loved her—he'd be asking was there gas in the car or did she want to go to Lou Tess to celebrate or would she brush her hair or something like that.

It scares me.

He leans down and kisses me on the mouth, quickly. "Come on," he says, "it's time for our show."

I walk with him, because he's holding my hand, and we go across the big stone-floored reception area, through an aisle made by the Friends who have all stepped out of the way, and the rest of the people who have finally got to crowd inside. Henry takes a pair of silver scissors somebody hands him and cuts a red ribbon that is across the doorway to a great big room called Contemporary Galleries.

. . .

Facing us is a free-standing panel that tells about the show. About Henry and all his other shows, and that this one is dedicated to his uncle, the original Henry Wozencrantz, a noted photographer, and next to that is one of his uncle's pictures, framed and hung, and I'm glad that Henry already showed me one, because otherwise it would be quite a start, seeing how much the woman does look like me. That reminds me, and I lift my head way up and push my shoulders back to imitate that long white neck.

To the left of the panel is a beautiful all-glass-and-metal elevator. You can look up and down to some of the polished brass machinery that must once have been part of the original brewery, and I think to myself that the elevator with its glimpse of a great gleaming world below is a work of art itself, and should have a label on it.

Then Henry turns me around, with everybody sort of standing there waiting—and I am staring at a six-foot-high picture of myself. Naked. Clear as day, down to the tiniest detail. I lose my breath as if I'd been hit in the stomach; I can't believe it.

It is one of the very first poses with the sheet around my middle and the hand, the first porcelain hand, between my breasts. It isn't in color exactly, but looks very much like the uncle's photographs, all in different shades of brown. And I remember something I didn't want to hear at the time, L.W. saying that Henry's paintings were like early daguerreotypes, and I see that is true.

Everything is clear as day and magnified besides: my breasts and how one is a little bigger, my shoulders which are thin and one is a little higher, the way my eyes turn slightly down at the corners, the little bit of flesh above each knee, the way my mouth looks when I am daydreaming. The way you can see the tip of my tongue.

Numb, not knowing what to do, feeling Henry holding tight to me the way you would hold a little kid in the middle of four-lane traffic, I read the card at the side of the picture.

Henry Wozencrantz (1942–   ), American
FEMALE MODEL, oil on canvas

(It is all in Spanish, too, naturally, so it also says MODELO FEM-ININA and so forth.)

With the crowd following us, we walk around the room slowly, and I can hear them all talking to each other, whispering mostly, and I can feel them staring at me—not me holding Henry's hand, but me up there, everywhere you look all over the walls.

I try to pretend I am not here.

(I lived a long time ago, maybe in some place like Paris. I lost my hand in an accident when I was a child. For a time I was the mistress of a photographer old enough to be my father, but then I ran away from him. I had to leave my hands behind.)

All twelve pictures in the room are me. There I am on the couch with the hand held between my thighs and I see with burning cheeks that my crotch which is about level with my real eyes is, in the picture, three times life size. Or more. I see, everyone sees, the smallest creases on my stomach, the chewed fingernails on my left hand, my dark round navel, and that disconnected, torn-loose hand all over me.

Henry is dragging me along, because I can hardly move, but he is not saying anything. People get in front of us, then realize where they are, who we are, and scoot out of the way. I don't know what Henry thinks; I don't know what I think. I am almost to the door, that's what I think: I've made it. I've seen them all and I've made it and I didn't run away, just like I promised him I wouldn't, and in one more minute I'm going to duck through that door and hide in the bathroom until all the Friends and their friends go home.

Then I am going to leave.

Leave Henry and San Antonio and my name and everything that anybody could ever recognize again. I'm going *home*, to Pass-of-the-Camels Park, to Beauregard Heights, to Honey Grove Hills, to Tierra Blanca Estates, where I belong. Back to the normal life with the oil rig salesman and the ice cream–eating babysitter. Back to adventure with Sears soaps and piano pupils and me answering to the name of Sonny.

I'm going to run away from all these people staring and staring at *Jolene*, and not a one of them will ever see me again, not ever.

36

I AM PULLING Henry along now, past the last awful one, through the curved brick archway, into another room with its cool stone floor. I glance about, looking for a way out, and then I see them. Four more walls in an even larger gallery, each hung with two or three or (the farthest wall) four pictures of me. There are the Indian blankets, with me naked in front of them, face pressed into the dyed wool, legs spread, braid down my back. There I am looking in the antler mirror. Wearing the turquoise necklace, the chaps, the spurs.

I want to cry out but no words come. I open my mouth

but I can't make a sound. I try to holler and a dry noise like paper crumbling is all that comes out.

I jerk my hand, resolved to leave it behind if Henry won't let go. When I get it free, I tear off the cape and stick the artificial hand, sheathed in its clammy glove, into his.

"Here, hang on to this."

"Don't," he says.

Everyone is behind us now, talking for all they're worth. I look back and see Karen, who knows that I am freaking out. I see Mrs. Wozencrantz, who is talking with her Hallie and Millie buddies and looking at her famous son's pictures as calmly as if they were a series on the uncompleted Fern Barn.

Then I see the stairs, steep and white.

"You promised," Henry shouts at me as I bolt.

But I am gone.

Up one flight to the European gallery, up another round of enameled metal to the Oriental gallery, up another—with the sound of someone, but, of course, Henry, behind me—to the Spanish floor. I am heading for the skywalk. I am heading for that tightrope of glass that will lead me over the center hall and the staring crowd below, down the other tower and out of the museum.

The skywalk seems miles long and I can see (down in the street) cars and, to the other side, more yellow brick buildings that must have been part of the old Lone Star Brewery, too. But I am not sightseeing; I am running as fast as seems safe with glass on both sides of me, four stories in the air. When I reach the second tower, I run down a hall and find the stairs to the floor marked Antiquities. It is a trap down here, however, because there are all the Near East pieces and they're all behind glass and walls, so there is nothing open but a narrow hall. I pass a women's bathroom, but am scared to go in; I know that when I come out there will be Henry, waiting.

I run down a flight and find myself in a room full of Mexican animals and ceremonial figures. There are dozens of them all around me: acrobats, dogs with hoops, monkeys with barrels, open cases of dance masks made of human hair, papier-mâché, leather, bone. There are sugar skulls. I mean to run on down and out of the building, but the room closes around me like a secret hiding place. I can stay and put on a jaguar's spots, a devil's horns, crocodile jaws. Suddenly, I don't want to leave.

It's foolish, with Henry pounding right behind me into the room, but I think that if only I can find the right face, the right magic clothes, then I can Purloin Letter it right in front of him and he will never see me.

I stand still, hiding behind a skeleton big as a man, with my arms at funny angles and my knees bent. I cover my face with a tiger's mask that has real boar bristles for whiskers.

Henry, winded, sits down between two other skeletons, part of a graveyard band.

"You promised," he says.

"I didn't leave."

"What do you call this?"

"I like this exhibit better. Better artists. I thought I'd be in this one instead."

"That hurts my feelings."

I make a tiger's growl.

Henry sighs and plays the drum of the skeleton beside him.

"You lied," I tell him.

"When I saw you, the resemblance, I couldn't think of anything but painting you. I was afraid if you knew what—"

"I'm going to cut them in little pieces and stuff all of them into Hefties and put them in the dumpster."

"They belong to me."

"I belong to me. Just because I let you dress me up and then undress me in public doesn't mean I'm yours. I get to say if I want to be naked as a jaybird three times larger than life all over eight walls in a public place. I get to say." By this time I am crying a lot and the inside of the tiger's mask is getting wet. I take it off. "I want to go."

"Then go."

"You'll try to stop me."

"Nobody will stop you any more."

"I don't believe you."

"What did your mom do when she smuggled you past your uncle and aunt?"

"You know." He isn't really asking. He knows. I've told him all those stories. "You know."

"I'm telling you no one can do that to you again."

"Right now that doesn't sound so bad."

"I've given you the cloak of invisibility. Fame."

I step out from behind the skeleton. I feel bone tired and my eyes are hot and red. "Then if you don't mind I'm just going to go right downstairs and out the door and head for home."

Henry plays a few notes on the drum. He gets up and dusts off his coat and tails. "Where's that?" he asks, handing me my cape, which has fallen to the floor.

37

"JESUS LOVES YOU," Mom said.

I was glad. I liked it whenever she decided that I could plug back into Sunday School.

This time we were living in Espiritu Santo Shores, a sub-

urb of Corpus Christi that Mom called the Holy Ghost outskirts of the Body of Christ.

We'd found the area while cruising up and down the Gulf
past Mustang and Padre islands, eating in diners, and picking
up postcards to send back to Brogan and Dad from Cow Trap,
Chigger, Chocolate, Blessing, Buckeye, North Pole, Gas Field,
and Flour Bluff. Mom had taken a liking to the religious atmosphere of the coast where every little wide spot in the road
had at least one white frame pitch-roofed Assembly of God
or boxy plain-windowed Church of Christ for every four families, maximum.

In our past moves, I'd already had a sampling of Sunday
Schools. I'd visited around among the denominations learning
who had robed choirs and who didn't even allow piano or
organs, who had altars and who had tables, who had grape
juice and who served wine, who had one God and who had
the Trinity, who sang songs you knew by heart and who had
hymns you could hardly move your lips to. I liked them all,
and missed the experience when I wasn't allowed to go.

But Mom—who wasn't of two minds about much of anything in this world—was of two minds about church. On the
positive side, she wanted me to be exposed, because, she said,
exposure to religion was a requirement for being a child, plus
also because she didn't want Dad going around saying she
was raising me a wanton heathen. On the negative side, she
considered that churches were, in the main and as a group,
composed of busybodies who were always wanting more information about you than you had the inclination to provide.

The problem was the Visitor's Card, which was always
present in the rack on the back of the chair or pew or bench
in front of you. Now the Visitor's Card was obligatory because
the people sitting on each side of you hadn't ever seen you
in their church before. And in the part of the service where
you turn and hug or shake hands, and say Hello or God loves

you to your neighbor, these people were going to indicate that you were a stranger in their midst. So if you'd already filled out your Visitor's Card, they could take a peek (or plan to take a peek later), and then they were relaxed about your being there and would automatically whisper helpful guidelines to you about the right way to do the holy rituals in their chosen place of worship. So they might indicate that the congregation always came in on the second stanza of the hymn after the choir sang the first verse by themselves, so you didn't blare out "This Is My Father's World" and humiliate yourself. Or that the tiny white pledge envelopes were also used for bills and coins so nobody got to see what anybody else put in the polished brass or sterling silver collection plate. Or that they were now using the new (or back to using the old) version of the Lord's Prayer or the Creed or the Confession of Faith that the elders or deacons or synod or mission had approved, so you'd know ahead all the niceties such as whether you'd be asking God to forgive your trespasses, or only your debts.

This time, when we lived in Espiritu Santo Shores, I got to go to Sunday School five weeks in a row, every week from right after Thanksgiving to Christmas.

Before our first Sunday there, Mom and I went through our usual practice session.

"We're the Galimatiases," Mom would say, or the Farfouillers, or the Desordonners. She had these French names that always made her crack up laughing, and she'd have me say them over until I had them right. No fractured French like Aunt Glenna's, she insisted, not from us.

Her theory was that picking an unusual name was far more convincing than saying you were Brown or Jones or Smith. Plus, if anyone asked if you were kin to someone they knew, whose name maybe sounded sort of like her made-up one, you could say that your family came from Chillicothe, and since nobody knew where it was, that put an end to that.

"We're the Enchevêtrers," she said, getting us ready. "Say it now. Now, say it again. Okay, now, What's your name, little girl?"

"Jolene Enchev-être." I always got to be Jolene, because Mom thought that me keeping my own name for Sunday School was a stabilizing factor.

"What's your mother's name?"

"Mrs. En-chev-être."

"Where do you live?"

"Uh—Corpus Christi?" Usually the rule was that we claimed the big city connected to our suburb, because it was safe to say El Paso or Texarkana but not Pass-of-the-Camels Park or Honey Grove Hills.

"Wrong, wrong, wrong."

But sometimes another line of reasoning was at work. It might be the big city was too small, too near, too familiar to our particular evangelical community, and then I was supposed to say the opposite side of the state. So in El Paso I could say, I'm from East Texas, and in Texarkana, I'm from West Texas, and in Tierra Blanca, I'm from South Texas. So on the Gulf I thought about that and answered, "North Texas, ma'am," and got Mom's toothy grin that meant that was the right answer.

"What brings you here today, Jolene?"

"Just visiting," I said, and then I waved an imaginary Visitor's Card in the air. She nodded, because that was usually the last question we got asked, before it was time to shake the preacher's hand and head out the door.

. . .

In the little farming community congregation we'd picked, it was the custom for each child on Christmas Eve to receive two gifts: a generic one, gender specific, from Santa, and a second, specially selected one, from her or his Sunday School teacher. That year was the only time I ever got my name on two presents under the tree, and the last time Mom ever let me go to church.

The Superintendent, all dressed up like Santa, called the names one by one, and all the boys got yo-yos and all the girls got tops (the stenciled metal humming kind that no girl wanted, and which the smartest ones quickly traded to unthinking boys for yo-yos). The class presents, in contrast, varied a lot. Some teachers were more thoughtful than others, some more knowledgeable, some more generous. Mine was all three. And since I'd been in Mrs. Jarvis's class for five Sundays, I was eligible for a gift. (A borderline situation, because children who suddenly appeared out of nowhere on the first of the four Sundays in Advent were usually suspect and told they would have to wait till next year.)

I'd seen two of the girls in my class—girls with the big wide freckled faces and plump trunks about to blossom out with breasts that were common for eleven-year-olds on the coast—get their names called once, for their humming tops, and then a second time, for, oh, miracle, not dime store hair barrettes, or lace handkerchiefs, or new toothbrushes, or Bible-story coloring books, but gold-toned lockets that really opened.

I could hardly believe it. It seemed too good to be true. That I was a full-fledged member of a Sunday School class, that Mom was actually letting me go to the Christmas drawing all by myself, that a gold locket just like that was about to be mine.

"Jo-lene," Mrs. Jarvis called out in her singsong voice, and I was halfway up the aisle with my hand out, wearing (I can still see it clear as day) a fuzzy pink junior-high-type sweater which just begged for a locket, when an arm slipped around my waist and Dad said in my ear: "Come on home, sweetheart, it's time you had a normal life."

And as we left the church, without my present, I remember thinking that if Jesus loved me so much how come He forgot to mention—Him, of all people, Who surely ought to know!—that it was the mistake of your life to answer to your name in public.

38

"FOR SLIGHTLY OVER three times the currently depressed price of this ranch-style, I could own a Soviet white fur coat," Glenna is saying.

"You and the Soviets are enjoying good relations? They're selling you clothes?" Brogan asks her.

"I'm reading from Neiman's Preview of Fall catalogue. It says that white full-sweep coats of natural lynx bellies are going for two hundred and ninety-five thousand dollars."

"The US of A they sell the bellies; the backs and feet and hands they sell their satellites."

"I'm just giving you a report on luxury spending to give an indication of the state of health of the dollar in Texas today, Brogan."

"Maybe they'll take your Joie de Beavre in trade. The Soviets are warming to trade."

. . .

For the last half hour I've been sitting out in front of their house, watching the sun shine through their live oak on the new-mowed lawn. In the early light the pink brick and gray shingled house with its wrought iron trim looks like it could be for sale, all fresh and unoccupied.

Funny, but I'd never noticed before the round white port-hole on the front that looks like a camera lens staring out. And that's a creepy coincidence, because I'd just gone by Hoyt and Cissy's place on Lot 4, Block 48—driven around the neighborhood of run-down houses on Plaza, Empire, Astoria, Jade, past all the little peeling lime green, coral, mustard homes with their palmettos and elephant ears and washed gravel roofs—and when I pulled up in front of theirs on Savoy, I saw that right on the porch, up the cement steps, was a round porthole window, looking straight at me.

I figured that Hoyt and Cissy were off at the bingo parlor and that I could slip in the back and never be noticed, jimmy open a screen if it was locked, kick over a rusted trike in the weeds—left from when Mom or Brogan was a kid. But the longer I sat, the more that round eye kept blinking at me, the more the sun and shadows kept shuttering it open and closed.

I don't know how come I never noticed it before.

That was earlier this morning. Last night I slept in the waiting room of Humana Hospital, along with about twenty other people. Nobody asked me who I'd come to see, even though I was wrapped in this long black thing like a Halloween costume six months early. I had to sign in, but I signed Jackson, figuring that every hospital in the world has a patient named Jackson.

It didn't actually turn out to be a bad place to stay; there was a bathroom right down the hall and I had cafeteria food last night and again this morning. I probably ate better than Mom, who was lying somewhere on the fourth floor—enjoying herself undergoing the treatment for pneumonia. It made me nervous, being that close to her, like she had eyes that could see through walls. It would soon be a week since the scam at the Fern Barn and I knew she'd be expecting me, but I was in no shape to decide how to hide two people; for now, it was all I could do to think about hiding one.

. . .

"Myself," Brogan says to Glenna, holding up the paper, "I've been reading the hot fresh news. For example, today the headline reads ALIEN SIGHTS UFO." He spells it out, s-i-g-h-t-s. "Now, they like variety in their coverage here. Yesterday, if I'm not mistaken, we had the big item top of page one informing us that UFO CITES ALIEN." He spells that, too, c-i-t-e-s. "Midweek, for a little change of pace, we'll get the articles on UFO SIGHTS ALIEN and ALIEN CITES UFO, if you follow me. And Sunday, the full banner spread, no initials—that's to aid your tourist—UNDERCOVER FEDERAL OFFICIAL CITES ILLEGAL ALIEN. Am I right?"

"Then why are you reading the paper, honey? Why are you right this very minute combing the newspaper if you know it by heart?"

"I was looking for a picture of Jolene," he says. "I was merely skimming the front section and the life-style, even though I happen to know that they put this paper to bed yesterday before lunch. That unless the president dies of old age, they don't add anything to this paper after lunchtime yesterday. But I happened to be taking a look is all."

Hearing that, I get a sinking feeling and step around the corner of the house.

"Here I am," I say.

"Jolene!" Glenna in her new pink warm-up suit bobs up in the air all excited, like I was somebody she never expected to see in her own backyard.

"Well, son of a gun," Brogan says. "Well, I declare. It's

Jolene herself, big as life." He wads up the paper and pulls out a wrought iron chair for me to sit in at the same instant that Glenna pours me a fresh glass of pineapple shake.

It gives me a scary feeling, to have them focusing on me that way, and I wonder what they know.

I don't have to wonder long, because Brogan is bursting with it. "We were sitting in the TV room, big as you please last evening, getting ourselves a little news along with a glass of Glenna Rosé—not the real thing, that's a few years away, but a sampling of what we intend to aim for, if you get my meaning, something classy from California, sampling the competition as it were—and there she was, our very own Jolene, *you*, looking like a movie star."

"Honey," Glenna elaborates, "they showed you turned sideways with that painter, both of you all dressed up—why, you're still in that black outfit, aren't you?—and with that makeup on, honey, you were the most beautiful thing we'd ever seen in our lives. And there were all those people in evening dresses crowding around you, why it was like looking at actors going into the Academy Awards ceremony with all those cameras flashing. When you said *model*—why, I never in all my born days imagined you meant that kind of model. Why, there was nothing else on the news hardly. Was there, Brogan? Was there anything else to amount to anything on the news?"

Brogan in his new gray warm-up suit is so agitated he can't stay still and gets up and begins to do a few deep knee bends and arm rotations. "Your aunt is not just talking local, either," he says. "She means your CBS, ABC, NBC, they all had this same shot of our niece that we raised, looking like maybe she had just stepped over the body of Brooke Shields or maybe Madonna, one of that kind, one of those yesterday folks who aren't today's news any more."

"And, honey," Glenna breaks in, jumping up herself and doing some waist bends. "They even showed a couple of the paintings, I mean not the whole things, not on TV, but just enough, your shoulders in one of them with you looking right out of the picture, and in another it was your hair in a pigtail and the camera went further down on that one, it being your back, down to your waist and it looked like you were on some kind of rug. Is that right? You would have thought you were the president of the United States the way all those cameras were flashing. I wonder if they had a plastic shield up when they were taking you, the way they do when the president travels. It's not really glass, so you can photograph right through it."

"It was a private party she was at," Brogan says. "No nuts were allowed. Unless you have a rich old lady nut with a bunch of diamonds on who had a gun in her girdle. Unless you had that kind of nut you didn't have a nut at that private party who was going to make you need a shield."

"I'm just saying. A celebrity isn't always safe." Glenna takes a big breath. "Honey, we could hardly sleep all night. Brogan wanted me to call you—he had it figured that you must be at Mr. Wozencrantz's house—but then we thought that wouldn't be right. We tried to get Hoyt and Cissy to ask did they see it, but they hadn't come home by midnight so we gave up. There didn't seem to be any point in telling your mother, sick as she is, and to tell the truth we got so excited we forgot to even go by during visitors' hours, but I guess she was hardly in a shape to notice. Or in telling your dad, either, him being on a rampage right at this time, and I certainly hope he was out showing samples and not parked in front of the evening news."

"I said to myself," Brogan interrupts, "that right there on my TV set was the very face to launch a thousand bottles of virgin-press Glenna Rosé. I said to myself, Brog, when the time comes, you've got prime advertising potential right here under your own roof."

"You'll be in all the papers, you know," Glenna says.

"Whatever is on TV always shows up in a couple of days in the papers."

I don't know what to say to them, although they may not be expecting me to say anything. After all, I never have said much around them; mostly I listened while they made their plans or had their discussions about what the true state of things was. Mostly they always liked to have a third party around, somebody they didn't really have to take much notice of, while they tried their ideas out.

It feels weird and awful to have them jumping around like they're doing and all the time keeping their eyes fixed on me, watching every move I make.

I finish my pineapple shake and get up to go in the house. I need to shower and to wash my hair, and to get out of this Dracula suit that I've been in for what seems like about four days spent with every hopeful and mourning family member in Humana Hospital.

"Hon." Glenna looks at me. "Why didn't you tell us? I mean, we would have kept it a secret. Why didn't you at least tell us, me and your uncle Brogan. You could have knocked me over with a feather; I thought I was going to faint on the spot, when I saw you large as life on that screen."

"Some things a person has to keep under wraps," Brogan explains to her. "Some things can't be unveiled until the time is right. You didn't see me announcing for example that my sign-up sheets at the gun-phone display had to do with another project that me and nobody else had occasion to know about."

I almost giggle at *under wraps* and *unveiled.* That's about the size of it, I think. I should have stayed under wraps and never unveiled in the first place. I should have stayed in the famous, wild-haired drama teacher's class and improvised my brains out. Give me another chance, watch, you can't believe how ready I am to be anything on wheels, a biscuit rising, the

color blue. If it's something else besides me, anything else,
I'm ready to go.

"I just wish you had told us," Glenna says again. "I'm not
fussing; just wishing that we'd been in on it."

Why didn't I tell them what? That I was off in a world of
my own about as safe as Daniel in the lions' den? "I need to
get out of this dress," I tell her now, because I can't think of
anything else to say.

"Well, sure, let me fill up the tub for you. Have yourself
a good soak. I've got bubble bath that's real nice. And bath
oil beads."

"Draw a bath, that's what you say," Brogan corrects her.
"You say, 'Let me draw you a bath.'"

"What's wrong with 'fill up the tub'? Jolene knows what
I'm talking about."

I can feel my skin crawl; it seems like I can't do anything
by myself any more. "That's okay," I say. "I know my way
around here." I laugh a little, to remind them that, after all,
I've lived here for half a dozen years.

"You want me to iron you something to wear? What about
makeup? Did you bring your things back with you? Is *he*—I
don't mean to pry, but is *he* going to pick you up here? Will
we get to meet him?"

Oh, Jesus, I wish I were back with the tiger mask on my
face or maybe behind the wooden crocodile snout, snapping
my hinged jaw.

Henry? I don't know if they'll get to meet Henry or not. I
don't know what I'm going to do about all my things over
there at his ordinary house which is less than a dozen blocks
away but that's something at least that I can keep either one
of them, or him, from finding out. Maybe that's what I should
concentrate on: getting out of this slice of the pie. It's getting
sticky in here.

Of all the times in my whole life for Mom to be taking a

health treatment, this is the worst. Think of a number between eighteen and twenty. That's me, Mom. Remember?
I'm the one who was in Mrs. Evans's class. Ridiculously,
knowing that Glenna and Brogan won't have an idea what
I'm doing, I hold up all the fingers on both hands and then
make fists and hold up all but one. Nineteen years old and
worse than an orphan. I've got foster families everywhere.

They think I'm exercising along with them, or stretching,
and before where they would have asked me, What on earth
are you doing? Got a cramp or something? now they just look
at me, like anything I'm doing must be the sort of thing that
a model who's on TV would do. And they don't have to understand it, because it's in another realm from theirs, it's part
of another, bigger world out there, with different rules.

Wouldn't you think that they'd want, at the least, to tan
my hide for appearing butt naked all over eight walls bigger
than life? In full view of, I was about to say, the whole collection of museum friends, but I guess the whole city is more
like it. Wouldn't you think?

"I just wish you'd told us, honey, that's all."

"Some things have to be kept under wraps, Glenna. I told
you. Now don't get on the girl, she needs to get herself fresh-
ened up and rested up. Go draw her a bath, like I said."

"I just want to know about her plans for the coming evening, if you don't mind. You don't mind if I ask you, do you,
honey?"

"I'm not going anywhere," I tell her. "I'm going to stay
here. Get to bed early."

"Not before we take you out for a proper dinner," Glenna
says and smiles real big at Brogan. "I mean, this is an occasion
that only comes once in a lifetime."

At that moment the phone rings.

"Excuse me a minute," she says, and puts on her secre-
tarial voice as she picks up the cordless phone. "Temple En-

terprises," she announces. Then her face breaks into a flutter of smiles and flushes as she listens. "Why, sure, she's right here. She's right here, sitting here with us. Why, of course you can." She covers the receiver with her hand and mouths to me: "It's *him!*"

Oh shit. How on earth? I guess it's not that hard. If my name's Temple and I have an uncle Brogan ... I guess it's not that hard. Then if Henry has any sense he'll know that it's just a stone's throw back down New Braunfels from his house to theirs. But then if he was going to show up—like Dad, like Mom—he'd have already done it, wouldn't he? He wouldn't be on the phone. Thinking about that, calming myself by reasoning that out, I say, "Hello."

"You need to call a reporter on the East Coast. He called here for you, but I didn't want to give him your number. With a number they can trace an address. That's why I didn't let them have a last name. Now I'm going to give you a number, call him collect—magazine reporters like to be called collect— and tell him the minimum you can. Don't say anything you don't want to read for the rest of your life. Say you modeled to save money for an acting career. Say you have an unlisted phone. Say you've been in a few college productions. Say you weren't born in this country. Say anything you want to that you can live with. Got that?"

"Do I have to call him?"

"If you don't, they'll make something up. They'll ask around. They'll print anything third-hand that makes good copy."

"You're just scared they'll call your mother and daughter."

"They already have. Mother can straight-arm a tractor. No problem. Karen told them she thought you were a costume-design major."

That makes me want to give the tan girl with the light

lashes a big hug. Costume design—that was quick thinking. It must have come from my being at her house pretending to be an antique dealer. But with a twist. I like that. I like it a lot. "Maybe I'll say that."

"Fine."

"I think I will. Acting they'll expect. Every model wants to get into film." I am surprised at myself for thinking so coolly about this. "I like costume-design major. Especially considering the costume work we did on the portraits." I say this with a serious tone and a straight face, and I can hear him laugh in a good way, like he's liking that and deciding that maybe I'm not permanently mad. Also, I can see that Glenna and Brogan are wanting me to sound like I know what I'm doing. That I have this wonderful thing going on that was a big project and a big surprise.

(They do not want me breaking into tears and throwing the cordless phone across the pink patio at the gray shingles, shouting at Henry that I'm not going to say a word to his creep reporter.)

"Portraits, that's good," he says. "Portraits of a student."

"From Chillicothe."

"Where?"

" 'The town where I live.' "

"Are you coming back here?"

"I don't know."

"I can't stand it without you."

"I imagine so." I say this in a light way, because Glenna and Brogan can only hear my end of the conversation.

"Will you call?" He sounds amused, and knows that I'm not alone. "The reporter?"

"Wait, I need a pen."

Glenna hands me her secretary's clipboard and ballpoint, tied on with a pink cord, for taking messages when she and Brogan are out on the patio or when she's under her home hair dryer or in the kitchen fixing a batch of milkshakes or some Snappy Tom on ice.

I write it all down and say to Henry before I hang up, "I need to have a little time alone," in a sweet way, so that Glenna and Brogan won't think that anything is wrong or that I'm raging angry at what Henry did to me. I don't want to give them that, any of them—not Henry and not them. I don't want them to know, not any of them, that it matters to me as much as it does. Once they see that, then they can't help it: no matter how well they mean or how much they want to be on your side, they use it. They see that torn open place and they are like dogs; they have to go for it.

"Come see me," Henry says, and hangs up the phone.

"I have to call *Newsweek*," I tell my aunt and uncle and watch their faces as they hear that. It is a piece of time that doesn't seem to move. I see them look at me through that fact: through *Newsweek* wanting me to call, and I know that it doesn't matter what I do any more, ever. They are never going to see me again except through that big glossy haze of *Newsweek* wanting me to call.

I do all right. Thanks to good old Karen, who was probably trying to send me a message of what to say so I wouldn't freak out. And I make a note that I'll pay her back somehow. You'd think if anybody would take the opportunity to say something really hateful, right in the reporter's ear, it would be Henry's daughter. But she didn't. Some people are a lot nicer than you would expect.

I call collect on the cordless phone, saying it is *Jolene* calling. The reporter sounds like he is about my age, although I know that can't be true. He wants some dirt or he wants some fascinating fact and it doesn't bother me a bit to tell him things that aren't true here in front of Brogan and Glenna, because they think that's part of talking to reporters. I give him the costume-design major stuff, and the growing up in

Chillicothe, which I have to spell. And then I tell him about how I wish to protect my family's privacy but that I can say they're in vineyards, that now that oil prices are down they've diversified into vineyards. And it looks like Brogan is going to have to cry. He has to do about ten deep knee bends and expand his chest and take a few arm swings, and look away for a minute.

Glenna leans forward, hardly able to stand not hearing it all. She tries to guess what they're asking me, putting it with what I'm saying, and I know she wishes she'd thought to go in the house on some excuse—to get us a refill on our health drinks or powder her nose or check on what's for lunch—so she could pick up one of the phones in the house and listen in.

What the reporter really wants to know is how do I feel about being buck naked all over the place, but I figure he can't ask outright, or put those pictures in either, because it's a family news magazine, so if I don't say anything that implies they're the way they are, then he can't do much with that. He asks me what was my reaction to the show. And I tell him that portrait painting is coming back, that art is back in the seventeenth century, hoping I've remembered the right stuff from what Mrs. Wozencrantz was saying to Hallie Fine Arts and Millie Bernais. I try to remember some of the names she mentioned (of artists then and now) but I can't. But I say it's a long tradition, portrait painting; that I'm glad to be a part of it. And then I get him off the phone. He's been panting a lot and I don't want to think about that part of it. A good reporter instead of a stringer would be more interested in Henry's technique. How did he make them look like old-fashioned photographs? And I wish I'd said something about that, but then I might have gotten in over my head, and, anyway, they must have talked to Henry, too, so he would have said all that. And about his uncle. I know he wants to give a lot of mention to his uncle.

I put the phone down in its cradle, so worn out I can hardly move a muscle. I do the ten fingers and then nine more, this time as sort of a joke to myself. "About that bath . . ." I say.

"You go right ahead." Glenna gives a little shake of excitement. "But now, honey, what I started to say before your call is that we are all going out to celebrate tonight, the three of us. We are going to have us a real first-class five-star dinner on the town. We, us, ourselves, are going to have dinner at *Lou Tess*."

"It's our treat," Brogan says. "It's on us."

"That's right." Glenna pulls something from her wallet and lays it on the table. "We have got here a brand-new unused maximum-limit MasterCard that we've been saving for something big. And this is it."

"Get your mouth to watering," Brogan says. "Anything on the menu."

"But right now," Glenna says, "I'm going to fill—"

"—draw—"

"—your tub."

"—her bath."

"Alien sights UFO," I tell them, saluting with a high five. And even though they don't understand what in the world my saying that has to do with anything at all that we've been talking about, they laugh. They laugh because they heard it from *Jolene*.

39

AFTER A FEW more days of being fussed over by Brogan and Glenna, I decide to try the Dawsons. Check out my options.

Driving down San Pedro, rounding the corner to Rosewood, I move in slow motion, relieved to be back in this part of town. Everything seems familiar in the way that suburbs did in the old days with Mom, and even though in this neighborhood each house is distinctive, with its eye-catching special feature, still these attention-getters give the houses a quality of sameness, of their own kind of protective coloration, the way that when you drive around a Heights or Hills or Park at Christmas, every yard has a Santa with reindeer and outdoor lights on all the shrubs, so that in one way each yard is different but in another way they're all alike.

I take my time at the mailbox with its lariat, the retama/huisache in the yard, the doorway lassoed in shellacked rope. I take my time pushing the doorbell, not really wanting to be inside so much as to be here right on this porch, someone who belongs here, ringing the bell, calling out. The yard and the porch and the door can be the whole stage set, for both acts. The Niece comes to the door; she waits on the porch. Years pass, the sun sets, she's under the tree in the yard. The moon rises, it's another evening, she's at the curb by her car.

L.W.'s mom answers my ring.

"Well, look here. Jolene," she says. "Buddy's out at school," she tells me before I can ask. "It's his play going on out there. You know about his play?"

"*The Second Peloponnesian War.*" I show that I do.

"That's it. That's what he said." She moves us both inside.

"Look who's here, Lenox," she calls out to L.W. Senior at the dining table.

He looks up, shifts his bulk. He is deep in the study of the Fixed Perpetual Calendar.

"Buddy's gone," he tells me, getting up like a gentleman. "He's not here. He's at the college."

"Trinity," Mrs. Dawson supplies.

"I know—" I am trying to think of a way to linger. "I was on my way to help with the play. But as I was driving up San Pedro from town, in a hurry, don't you know, to get there in plenty of time, well, see, I got something in my eye." I squint and pull down my lid over my lower lashes, hoping it will look convincing. Hoping a slight wetness will result. I blink quickly two or three times. "I wonder, it isn't safe, you know, driving with something in your eye, if I could rinse it out, if it would be trouble for you . . ."

"You come right on back. Use the guest towels. Cold water is the best," Mrs. L.W. says.

"You have to watch yourself out there," Mr. Dawson advises.

"Maybe a little boric acid?" she suggests.

"Driving down the street is a hazard these days," he says.

"You just come right on in here." Mrs. Dawson leads the way to the bathroom off the hall, the bathroom between the living room and L.W.'s bedroom.

"I appreciate it," I tell her.

Left alone I lean against the wall, almost weak with relief at how here, at least, things are the same. I never want to leave. I let the water run slowly, splashing it with my fingers from time to time, listening to the comforting sounds. I can hear Mrs. Dawson spit on the iron, can hear the thump of the heavy metal hitting the starched cotton dress, red and white, pulled over the covered ironing board. Spit, slap, it makes a good rhythm.

Owning Jolene

I hear L.W.'s dad pull out his chair, get settled, scoot the chair back to the table, shuffle sheets of charts across the waxed surface.

Why wouldn't it be all right for me to go into the kitchen and make those chocolate chip cookies, careful to rotate the hot metal sheets back to front and top shelf to bottom for even baking, the chocolate and condensed milk and pecans all heating up and running together into a rich dark batter?

I splash a little tap water on the back of my neck, resolved to ask them if I can just lie down for a minute. Just lie there for a minute in L.W.'s room, on his neat single bed, beneath the hanging mitts and hats.

Then I hear Mrs. Dawson whisper, "She looks just the same as she did on TV, doesn't she, Dad? The image. I declare I couldn't believe my eyes. *Jolene!* Right here at the door."

"You don't have to tell me what I already know. I know what I'm seeing when I'm seeing it. I'm seeing what I saw on my TV set and in my newspaper. The very same. Prettier in the flesh if you ask me."

"Won't Buddy be sick to miss her."

"Not safe out there by herself. Where's her folks should be carrying her where she needs to go?"

Then I do feel sick and want to lie down—but not here. Not here where I have already disturbed the natural order of things. I turn off the water and strain for the sound of L.W.'s mom spitting on the iron, that nice sizzling sound.

"Hush," she whispers. "Here she comes."

"I'll be on my way," I tell them, opening my eyes wide to show that everything is fine.

"You'll be going on to the school now, won't you?"

"I'm on my way. Thanks a lot. I sure appreciate your letting me stop by."

"You come again now. Any time. You come back to see us anytime you feel like it."

In the yard I look back at the safe-house set.

It isn't very good; you can see the joints where the flats hook together. And the porch: it's flimsy, almost cardboard. It doesn't look like anybody really stands there and rings the bell. But the rope—I wipe my eyes—the rope around the door, that's good. And the matching one on the mailbox, that's good, too.

40

*I*T ISN'T HARD to find the theatre building at Trinity. There are posters about coming performances and even a marquee in front. But I'm not in a big hurry; I figure that just about now the crew and cast will be having tacos and burgers from bags backstage and having their opening night pep talk. I have a clear picture of that, although I've never been part of a play. A lot of stuff like that you get in your mind from films. Besides, my famous teacher liked to talk about tragedies she'd played in capitals around the world.

I sit in the courtyard by the drama building on a slatted redwood chair, one of a dozen set in a circle around a redwood table, near square hedges and round flower beds, all dappled by a live oak in the low setting sun. Probably some talk session has taken place here, with some other famous teacher, explaining the message of a play or the concept of a role. Or maybe just actors offstage talking about was it okay to sit around in a place this luxurious and landscaped, did that count as being serious and in class?

I know it isn't true that only rich kids come here—because L.W. and the Pal are here. But then maybe they let in talent at the top, to make a good impression, the way you see foreign students, wearing different clothes and sounding different, asking you the way to the administration building.

Once inside, I go in the theatre, and it is a big splendid room with soft black-tweed seats fanned out in a semicircle, rising up in steep rows. But the stage, which has a few black cube tables and black chairs and a black baby grand piano is deserted. It isn't actually a set; there are blank gray flats in the back and a few chalk marks on the floor. Nobody is in here.

I look around, thinking there should be people running up and down the aisles, noises off in the wings. It is like a model of a theatre, beautiful in all its blacks and grays, but it doesn't look as if anyone has ever been in here. Maybe it's new; maybe even the chalk marks are part of the action.

I sit a minute, trying to imagine a play here, someone saying lines, lights from the spots showing up a face, the face of a girl caught in a crowd, a lot of voices and people waving cameras—but that's been done before.

Finally I leave the quiet and go back out into the entrance hall. I wander around until I see a sign that says WORKSHOP THEATRE and an arrow that points down a narrower hall.

There it is. A big three-color poster with very arty graphics that spell out THE SECOND PELOPONNESIAN WAR. A TWO-ACT PLAY. BY LENOX WORTH DAWSON. The last letters of the title and his name are made very big and set at an angle, so you have E D N R and X H N leaping out from the sign. It's very effective. Something about it has a Mexican air and I wonder if L.W. got to do his own designing or, in a workshop play, if there is a crew for that.

I open the door a crack and there it is. His play. No mistaking it. The set is an intersection. High up are two street signs: HUISACHE and RETAMA. Below each sign is a smaller one pointing to the left and right respectively, and these, being in

English and then Spanish give the idea right away what the play's about. Under HUISACHE an arrow indicates EL SENDERO DE LA CRUZ ASAMBLEAS DE DIOS, and, under RETAMA an arrow points to THE WAY OF THE CROSS ASSEMBLY OF GOD.

I feel better already, tucked here under L.W.'s Brown Umbrella. I figure if he can't get his mind off the problem even when I'm sitting on his bed, then he's sure not going to be noticing me here.

A lot of kids are shouting and lights are changing colors and it's hard to tell who is part of the play and who is part of the audience—but there may be a lot of duplication.

You can tell it's a workshop because there is paint on the floor and stacks of flats against one wall and some unlabeled boxes tied with string.

I take a seat in the back on one of the folding chairs that are all on one level and arranged in straight rows with a wide aisle in the middle. It is dark back here; the houselights have suddenly dimmed, and I feel as inconspicuous as I have anywhere since before Henry's show.

Maybe I'll just spend a lot of time the next few years sitting in the back of theatres around town, being part of the audience for tryouts and readings and rehearsals, clapping when everybody else does, getting up when it's over and wrapping a scarf around my neck and pulling on an acid-washed jean jacket when everybody else does, or coming in shorts and a T, if it's that kind of crowd.

I'm in my poet's skirt, with my gauzy blouse made in the Philippines, and it seems to me that it's been about a hundred years since I made up my rice-white cheeks and went in search of a Texas Ex at that first party where I met L.W. I wonder what would have happened if I'd gone home with him that night; if everything would have turned out differently.

I remember later times, too, when things could have gone either way. The red panties tucked under his pillow in that house on Rosewood with its arched doorway, its nailed-shut windows in back, its big yard dotted with blackbirds, its green-barked tree by the walk. I remember our improvising that I'd been attacked by a mugger in the parking lot outside Al's diner. Would we have been any different with each other if his folks had stayed away an hour longer? If the Pal had waited till another day?

If I hadn't been already posing for Henry?

I wish for a minute that it was me up there standing at the intersection, sleeves rolled up, my back turned, looking first toward EL SENDERO DE LA CRUZ and then toward THE WAY OF THE CROSS.

L.W. turns around to scattered applause. He looks to his right and then his left, and while he's looking right another figure in pants and shirt with rolled-up sleeves enters on the left. It's the Pal, dressed with her hair tucked up and a cap on and wearing suspenders like a man. They slap hands and then both look right and left. Clearly they are waiting for someone.

Arch has a sign that she swings that identifies her as a member of OBEMLA (Office of Bilingual Education and Minority Languages); L.W. waves a similar one that says U.S. ENGLISH (the one-language lobby).

Finally, the main character rushes in from the right, dressed in workman's coveralls that say FIRE ANT CONTROL across the chest. He holds up a placard on which is lettered LULAC—a prop that lets everybody know he's a member of the League of United Latin American Citizens. They both greet him, and then we know that his name is Jesús, and this is part of the point, too, because he's called *Geez-us* by L.W. and *Hey-soose* by Arch.

From then on, it doesn't matter what any of them say. We know what the play is about.

But L.W. makes a lot of speeches about how bilingual education can isolate non–English-speaking children for years and that such programs are certain to produce a new form of separate but equal education, and separate is not equal.

Archie argues back, saying that one-language efforts are racist and part of fear-mongering tactics designed to destroy the values and language-of-origin of immigrants.

Heysoose/Geezus doesn't get to talk about the topic. To show that his main concern is economic—the cash language—he talks a lot about fire ant control. And whole riffs sound familiar to me: "For your pasture and rangeland, even your vegetable garden, my product is fire ant specific. It has no effect on native ants, no effect whatsoever on honey bees, it also has no effect, guaranteed, on aquatics or mammals. My insect growth regulator imbedded in defatted grits has a half-life of thirty years, works up to ten years, and eighty pounds per acre broadcast reduces the population effectively." (And then I know why L.W. didn't get mad at me for dashing out of Brogan's party: he was getting material for his play.)

I think about Henry, who I'm beginning to miss, and his daddy, Red, who could hardly read and write, and it seems to me that maybe *any* language is a cash language, compared to not having one at all.

L.W. and Arch work well together; they have rehearsed and rehearsed and you can tell they've forgotten that the rest of us are even here, because they are having such a really good time hearing their worked-over lines in performance.

The trouble is that the hero, who is supposed, naturally, to be a Chicano, is actually an American Indian student who doesn't know a word of Spanish. So that whenever he has to give a few phrases in his "own language" they are labored and halting and everybody snickers. Or they start to, but then stop because they don't want to seem anti-Hispanic.

At the last, L.W. and Arch have declared a truce and are standing arm in arm. Looking at the guy in coveralls, Arch

says, Hey-soose speaks both languages. To which L.W., looking toward the two churches, replies, Geez-us speaks both
languages, too.

At that point the hero walks to the front of the stage and
delivers the final line: I thank you both for your help but I
must resolve this battle of the tongues myself.

Then the lights go down to let us know the curtain is
falling, and L.W. and Arch are back where they started, signs
held high, at the crossroads.

"Author, author," call out a couple of chums of L.W.'s
and "Hero, hero," holler a few friends of the Indian's.

Someone says, "Archie, take a bow."

She obliges, leaning forward on the edge of the workshop
stage, staring into semidarkness. Suddenly she spots me and
straightens up. "Jolene," she yells. "Look, L.W., it's *Jolene.*"

All the audience of about thirty kids turn around and stare.
The houselights come up bright.

"No kidding," someone says.

"Wow."

"Hey."

"It's *her.*"

Archie goes backstage and reappears waving a copy of
Newsweek—with my photo on the cover.

. . .

I think about falling through the floor. I didn't know. I never
thought to look on the newsstand. Why should I? I see it
across a lot of people who are getting in the way, but I can
make out bare shoulders with JOLENE in black letters, and then,
under the hand I'm holding, THE RETURN OF THE LIVE MODEL.

L.W. and Archie, still dressed as the Czech and the German, jump down off the stage and head in my direction, and
Hey-soose, who doesn't know what's going on but doesn't
want to be left out, comes along, too.

The Pal looks about to pop with excitement. Like maybe this is the greatest thing ever to happen in her life. She says she's the one who found the magazine. That she was walking around the shopping center, going past Taco Cabaña and the Four Seasons: Mustard, Mayo, Catsup, A-1, and then past Handy Andy and Walgreen's, and she went in to buy some dental floss and the first thing she saw was a stack of *Newsweek*s with my picture on it, being unpacked. Well, she looked twice, she says, and just about had a fit. I know her, she told everybody, and bought two copies. One for her, and one for L.W.

"Why didn't you let us know about your show at Fine Arts?" L.W. asks. "It's terrific. We went by to see it. I'm really glad you could come to the play. I was going to let you know about opening night, but I didn't have an address. I mean this is really great." He turns around and introduces the crew to me. "This is Lights," he says, pulling a tall boy forward. "This is Sound. And this one, come on, don't hide back there, this is the person who did the fantastic set."

"I liked it a lot," I say to Stage Set.

"Thanks." The black girl smiles.

"I liked the play, L.W. I could see a lot of stuff you talked about in there. A lot of the business about the problem of bilingual education."

"You did? You really did? That's great. Maybe you can get me a national review. Ha, ha, I mean it. That's great, having somebody like you like it and pass the word on. That could really be a break. Arch did all the dirty work," he says. "Arch wrote the hard parts."

She laughs and says that it was him who had the idea in the first place.

She asks me, "How's it feel, seeing all these pictures of yourself in print?" She flips the magazine open to a two-page spread. "I mean they're fantastic. You really look beautiful and I guess you'll get calls from all over the country. Gosh, that must be something, having that happen to you. Maybe it doesn't seem all that special to you, I guess if you're used to it, used to seeing yourself everywhere, you know, like on billboards or something. But it seems to me like you'd be on top of the world."

"Look," L.W. says, "we're having a cast party. Well, I mean cast and crew, not just the three of us, ha, ha, at Zona Rosa. And, say, you're wearing that poet outfit, that's great. I mean going back to Zona Rosa just like the first time. Hey, everybody—I met Jolene at Zona Rosa, how about that?"

All the kids look at me and at L.W. who knows me. Some of the students who held back while he and Arch were talking to me now move forward. They move forward in a crush and for a minute they get between me and the *Peloponnesian* players.

It hurts, L.W.'s treating me like this. Like somebody he's never seen in his life; somebody he's heard about on TV. It was one thing, not that I got used to it, for Brogan and Glenna to act differently, because I figured it had to do with their thinking my being famous rubbed off on them. But I thought L.W. would be the one person in the world who would understand about the show—that it was all *out there,* the way it was when we were being the model and the broker for the cellular clients. But when the students clear a path and I'm in his line of vision again, I can see he isn't looking at me the same way any more.

Actors meet only on the stage, I told him once. Now I can see it's true.

"Excuse me," I say, remembering some unfinished business, "I have to make a phone call."

41

"THINK OF A NUMBER between nine and eleven," I say into the receiver. My mind is back where it belongs: on retrieving Mom.

"Ten," she says faintly, her tone rising with interest. "Ten. Where's a clock? They don't give you a clock. There must be a clock in this morgue."

"This is your sister-in-law talking to you," I say, "this is not your daughter Jolene. This is not me. I'm asking you, Did you get the flowers?"

"Glenna. You're Glenna."

"That's right. Are you nodding your head yes?"

"I got the flowers," she says. "Real beauties they are. I've never in my life seen quite such beautiful potted mums, just exactly that shade of pink."

Same old Mom; improvising just to flex her talent.

"Are you listening?" I ask her.

"Sure am," she says, her voice stronger. "Sure am. Surely am grateful for this great big beautiful pot of potted mums in this shade of lavender-pink that I'm sure is one of a kind. I don't believe I've ever seen it before, not in all my born days."

"Okay. Have on minimum clothes when I come. Got that?"

"I sure do. I sure do appreciate, Glenna, your thinking of—"

"Get the nurse in there for something. Coke, trip to the bathroom, Kleenex, aspirin, something. Have her come in and keep her there a while, so she's just been to see you. Got that?"

"Not many family members would do such a thoughtful thing as you did, sending this pot of potted pinky-purple mums, I mean that truly. I really appreciate—" And at that her voice cracks just the least little bit, chokes up just a little. An old trouper, out of practice.

" 'Bye," I say.

She's still carrying on about the mums as I hang up the phone.

.   .   .

I find L.W. and Archie, who are waiting for me, and apologize for taking so long. "Sorry," I tell them, "my mom's been real sick. Listen, I'll meet you at Zona Rosa. That's great, old times and all. We'll celebrate. But you all go on. I've got to run by the hospital first."

"Gee, I'm sorry to hear that, about your mother." The Pal is relieved that things are okay, that she didn't do something to chase me away.

"Oh, it's not real serious. But, pneumonia, that can be— well, anyway, you all go on."

"You sure?" L.W. is not convinced. He must be remembering that I said my folks were separated and moved around a lot. Maybe he thinks I'm making this up about Mom. I can see he's trying to measure this against my past performances: the poet, the broker, the niece. He takes a close look. He notices that I've put on a lot of mascara since I ducked out; that I've added a lot of blusher. He computes that, and decides that I'm getting the feel of a new role, Artist's Model.

I like that. For one thing, it's true more or less. For another, his thinking that plays right into my plans.

"We're not going to change," he tells me, in case I was thinking about putting on something fancy.

"Good." I adjust the shoulders of my gauzy blouse as if to say that I'm going to go in these same clothes, but maybe with just a few embellishments. I try to recall what he said at the diner when I told him I was going to be a fashion model at Glenna and Brogan's car-phone party. He said I had the cool look, that was it. So I try to project cool.

"You sure you don't want us to wait for you?" L.W. asks.

"No. I just had to call the nurse's station, to make sure it wasn't too late to stop by. You all go on."

I hesitate a minute, making sure that he's not sure, that he doesn't quite believe me. Then, as he turns to go, with Archie and Lights and Sound and Stage Set and the Indian who played Jesús already ahead of him, calling, Come on, let's go, I pull him toward me and whisper, "I'd like about four minutes in the prop room. I'd like, you know, to go through the wardrobe trunks." I act embarrassed, look down and then away, as if this new role is going to take a bit more disguise than I've got.

"Oh, hey, that's— Sure. Sure." He nods, catching on. "Arch, you go on and wait for me at the car. We'll caravan downtown. Not all of them know the way. I'll just be a sec."

He steers me back inside the dark workshop theatre, turns on a small exit light, then shows me how to go up on the stage. Behind the flats are a few footlockers and some hanging stuff, like the racks that people check their coats on in restaurants.

"This is all we've got. Mostly we just wear our own clothes or borrow what we need, like we did tonight. Except the caps; they were still here from *Waiting for Lefty* that they did last year. But anything you see, I mean this is all contributed. You don't want a real costume, do you?"

"No, you know, just something that will give me—" I reach down and pull up a length of yellowed lace and try it on like a shawl.

"Sure," he says. "I got it. Just close the door after you. It's great you could come, no kidding."

"Thanks. Thanks for everything." I give him a good-bye kiss on the cheek, because this is it, whether he knows it or not.

. . .

Alone, I try to think. A hat, that's the main thing. And a man's suit, or, styles being the way they are, a jacket and trousers, not matching. I find an old pair of pleated pants, from somebody's daddy. They have a couple of moth holes in the cuffs, but who'll be looking that close? Fortunately, the rumpled look is in. I root around for a man's plaid jacket, but no luck. Then for any jacket at all. I find a sweater, a turtleneck in a dull gold color. But no jacket. Finally, I find the top of a tuxedo. I look at it and decide it will have to do. The hat is no problem; there is a trunk full of hats. I guess they're the major prop for changing roles in a hurry. I take a man's felt and then glance around for shoes and socks. But of course actors use their own, and besides, who wears socks any more anyway?

We'll go with what we've got.

I'm off the stage and to the door when I go back and grab one of those cardboard suitcases used in plays by all departing husbands, traveling salesmen, and con artists.

Perfect.

42

I GO IN GENERIC. Who expects a celebrity to observe the rules?

Getting off the mud-colored elevator on the fourth floor, I gaze at the burlap-plastered walls and get my bearings. I got Mom's room number from the desk downstairs; I know where the rest rooms are located from my night in residence on the black vinyl waiting-room couch. When I saunter up to the nurse's desk, the LVN on duty is reading, what else, a copy of *Newsweek*. Everything is going fine.

"Excuse me," I say.

"Visiting hours are over." She doesn't look up. Her magazine is open to the article about how artists are all using live models again. On one page a naked child is curled up on the floor by a giant plant and a man's coat; facing that is me, holding the severed hand.

"I'm Jolene," I tell her. "The model."

She looks up. "Visiting hours are—" she stares at me and then down at the page. "Fantastic!"

"Please. My mother is a patient here."

She looks again. "Wait'll I tell my boyfriend."

"I just want to check on her; I won't be a minute."

"Well, it's against the rules, but, well, look—you can't stay long."

"Temple. Her name is Midge Temple."

"Temple, Temple, here we are." She reads the chart and points the way. "That's room 408, down there."

"Thanks a lot."

"I was just in there," she confides. "Her blood count's fine, but she still has the cough and weakness. It can take a while. I bet she'll be ready to go home in a few more days." She points again. "I'd take you down, but I'm not supposed to leave my station—"

"I can find it. Thanks so much." I take about four steps, then look all around, and walk back to her. "I'm sorry to bother you again, but is there a men's room up here?"

"What'd you want that for?"

"Oh, I came with my agent. He wouldn't wait downstairs. I think he's scared of hospitals; you know how some menare."

"You're telling me."

"So I let him ride up in the elevator with me, and made

him promise to stand right over there and wait." I make a big point of looking around in all directions. "But now he's disappeared."

"I expect that's where he went. It's over there, down that hall." She lowers her voice. "Is he old or something?"

"He's old, but that's not it, if you mean his having a retention problem or something. I think they, you know, people like that, booking agents, I think maybe they're doing something else in the men's room."

"You don't mean—?" She looks horrified.

"Oh, not sex. I meant, you know, up his nose—" I make a gesture, like I'd ever seen that done. Gambling on the chance that what she and I know about serious use of recreational drugs we got from the same place: films.

"I hope nobody walks in there on him. They'll have my head for sure."

"Listen, I'm sorry."

"Don't worry." She remembers who she's talking to and adds this to the story she'll tell. "Nobody up here at this hour. Doctors been gone since supper. I'll keep my eye out. You just go right on down there and see your mother."

"I appreciate it." I lift the suitcase so she can see it. "I brought her a new gown. There's not much you can bring a sick person."

"That was nice."

I trot down the hall, looking back over my shoulder a couple of times, as if I'm trying to catch a glimpse of the drug-freak agent who naturally goes everywhere with me, me being a celebrity, and then turn sharp as a knife into Mom's room.

.   .   .

The clock on her wall (big as a pie plate and facing her bed) says exactly ten o'clock.

She's sitting up, her hair tucked under a shower cap, dark glasses on, and not a stitch of clothes.

"Good girl," she says when she sees me. "I figured you'd wait for today; not too many family members crawling the halls. Good thinking."

"Did you eat?"

"Every last thing on the supper tray. They've got me on a liquid diet. Liquid diet in case you don't know means a bowl of Jell-O and two cold poached eggs that stare up at you like cow eyes. And one bitty tiny glass of pineapple juice. If you call that a meal, then I ate."

"Did you pee? We've just got about five minutes."

"Yes, indeed. Made a big production out of it. Fluid in and fluid out, I told her. Made a big production and leaned on the LVN like a big ton of old straw so she'd get the point of how helpless the woman in 408 was at this time."

"Great. Now here's the plan." I unpack the suitcase while telling her about the missing agent in the men's room.

"Now here's what you do," I say. "Are you listening?"

"I'm all ears."

"Here's what you do. You get into these clothes—they're the best I could find. You get into these clothes and back out the door of this room, so if the woman in white looks up you're going to look like you were trying to come *into* the room and that I'm pushing you out of it. Got that?"

"Got it." Mom is now standing on the floor, spry as can be, pawing over the garments. She pulls the trousers on over some panties she's fished out of a drawer in the bedside stand. She pulls on the turtleneck over a bra she materializes from her purse which hangs on a hook inside the closet door.

It's a double room, and all this time some other patient two feet away, whom we can't see because the white curtain is completely wrapped around her bed, is wheezing and moaning.

"Don't bother about her," Mom says, waving her away. "She's a terminal."

Mom puts on the tux jacket, sees the problem, rolls the sleeves up almost to the elbow in the trendy style, and turns the collar up as well. The icing on the cake, she takes an eyebrow pencil from her bag and makes stubble on her chin and upper lip with quick flawless jabs not even bothering to look in a mirror.

"You'll have to wear your own shoes."

"No problem." And of course there's not, because she never owned a pair of heels and these are basic flats, definitely gender-general shoes, the next thing to loafers.

"That's good." I hand her the hat, fascinated at how her old tricks take right over. She's back and ready to go on; she hears the sound of music and the rustling of the audience. What a ham, my mom. What a performer. "Now here's what we're going to do," I say, as she shoves the hat down tight, puts the shower cap back in the drawer, the shades back on.

"What? What are we going to do?"

While I admire her attire, she scratches herself under one arm, with the other folded across her chest. She's the best.

"What we're going to do is, you're going to back out that door—"

"Don't repeat yourself, Jolene."

"And then you're going to turn toward the nurse's station and grab your wienie, got it? The nurse is thinking that I've been visiting my mom here, and you're going to grab your wienie because you're the old man, the snorting agent who's just come out of the bathroom. And then we're going to march right to the elevator an hour after visiting hours are over and Purloin Letter it right out the front door."

"What's holding us up?"

In the hall, I wave at the LVN who puts her finger down on the page to mark the spot and waves back. She stares at me to get it in her mind that sure enough it's me, right here in Humana Hospital, on an ordinary night when she was just marking time. A big event right here on her shift.

"Your mother okay?" she asks, just to remind me that she's bent the rules a tad.

"She's fine. She liked the gown, she liked the color, but she was half asleep."

"You found your friend, I see," she says, making a gesture in the direction of my booking agent, who is holding himself and hop-skipping along, in a real hurry, scared to death to be in a hospital.

"He tried to follow me in her room, but I didn't let him in. Who knows what he might have—"

"You're telling me."

"Thanks again."

"Sure, *Jolene.*"

.   .   .

I have a little delay with the getaway, because Mom wants to keep watching how the emergency room doors fly open every time a car wheels up the steep drive, but even so I figure that by the time somebody brings around the sleeping pill to the woman in 408, we'll be heading up Broadway, through Brogan's piece of the pie on our way back to home plate: Lot 4, Block 48.

I have to detour once at Stop-N-Go to make a phone call, but that doesn't take long, and while I'm there I grab some of her favorites: Oreos, Fritos, a Baby Ruth, and a Dr. Pepper to wash it down with.

"Supplies," I tell her.

She takes to the treats like a dog to a sirloin strip and before my eyes the color comes back to her face.

"Brogan says you're famous." She wipes her mouth, still in her hat.

"That's what I hear."

"You're cased on coverall."

"So they tell me."

"Well," she says, "early training."

"Where've you been living?" I ask.

"Here and there." She's cautious out of habit. "One place and another."

"Like old times."

"Wrong. Definitely wrong. Not like old times. Old times people liked their girls to play piano, boys, too, headed for the concert stage. Liked them to learn the scales. To learn their fingering. Every Good Boy Does Fine. Good Boys Do Fine Always. E,G,B,D,F; G,B,D,F,A. Now they're not interested. Piano lessons? What's a piano? What's a lesson? You must be kidding, Mrs. Temple. Pay money to learn to count one-and, two-and, three-and, four-and? That's straight out of weird, Mrs. Temple."

"So what've you been doing?"

Mom bites her lip; looking like a man in a turtleneck and wrinkled tux coat who wishes he had a fix. "You wouldn't believe."

"You're versatile."

"Church organist. Masonic dances. I was almost down to public school." She sniffles but then gets a grip on herself and polishes off her candy bar.

When we pull into the old neighborhood, going down Empire past Jade, turning onto Astoria, back to the old place on Savoy, she whimpers slightly, and I can't tell if she is relieved or sad or both to be back.

The lime green asbestos-siding house with its peeping porthole looks the same as when I was here last: no FOR SALE sign in the yard; trash bags piled up at the curb; circulars spilling out of the mailbox.

"Hoyt and Cissy'll rat to Brogan where I am," Mom mentions.

I don't say that it doesn't matter any more who knows where she is. That we won't be playing that game any more. Because I know she doesn't see that after a while escape takes on a life of its own; that after a while you're not running *from*, you're just running.

"They're off playing bingo," I tell her.

"You know that or you're guessing?"

"Guessing."

"Good guess. Come on, I'll show you where they hide the key."

In the old days when we lived here, Mom would always leave me to wait in the front by the drooping elephant ears. Then she'd come back, waving the key in her hand, saying, "What you don't know you can't tell a certain interested party who might be nosing around."

This time she leads me to the backyard and lifts up a rubber mat that's lying beside the sweet gum. Under which the grass has long since died. There on the ground is a house key, tied with a twistie to a beer can pull. "*Vole-la*," Mom says, back in good spirits, imitating Glenna's French.

She unlocks the door, puts the key back under the rubber mat with the pill bugs. Inside, she looks around the kitchen. The breakfast dishes are on the oilcloth-covered table. Coffee grounds are in the sink. It smells of cigarette smoke.

"Same old place," she says, looking glad. She gives me a squeeze and then flaps her tuxedo jacket like bat wings and dances a little two-step in her pleated prop-room pants.

I put on some coffee. Thinking it's late; that I should just make up a bed for Mom.

But when I go to look for her, she's rummaging happily in the storage room off the back bedroom.

"Amazing treasures here." She gestures to the string-tied boxes and piles of clothes. "I guess every week of my past life is right here, filed away, waiting for me to dig it out. If I want, say, the program from the exact Valentine's Day sock hop of my senior year, well, here it is."

Tired of her agent's role, she changes into a silky dress with a white collar that must have been hers in the past, as it's too big ever to have fit Cissy. It looks good, being a sort of dressy seaweed green with a lot of dots and bows. She finger-combs her hair, puts on some bedroom slippers, and continues to dig.

"And what have we here? I declare. This is right back in style. Look at that. See that hemline? See those shoulders? A little musty. Is that a hole? No, I think that's just a spot. Nothing to it. And dishes—I wonder if they have a dish elf that lives in this room making these sets of plastic dishes the way the shoemaker's elf made shoes. I might just take myself a set, I'm down to a few essentials right now.

"If and when I get my car in working order—that's how come I dumped myself on Brogan's lap at that greenhouse, I'd run out of gas in several respects—I'll be on my way. You can't be in my business trucking around on foot. You can't be in my business and be stuck on public transportation either because 'burbs don't have public transit, that's how you know they're 'burbs: they depend on cars for their existence.

"Look at this, Jolene, look at this. A bird cage. From before you were even born. I think I may take this. Living alone I get lonesome without somebody to talk to. A bird is a nice thing to have, stays where you put it, uses the newspaper, sings a little, or that kind they used to have—budgies—talks to you. I'll get myself a budgie. Teach it to say: 'I see a piano teacher.' And what's this? Would you believe. Under all this stack of papers, the good old World Books. I'm traveling light; I'll just pack them up and take them along. It never hurts to have information at your fingertips."

That's my cue to exit, when Mom starts planning her next move.

I slip out front, look up and down the street, then stop just long enough to tie one of Hoyt's white handkerchiefs to the front porch rail.

43

J——

Smart cookie, you are.

Arranging a reconciliation.

Me turning around expecting it to be you, Jolene, standing there and instead there was Turk Jackson, your dad, looking like he'd seen a ghost. Me. Wearing the green polka-dotted dress that I was wearing the very first time he laid eyes on me.

I felt like I'd seen a ghost myself.

It was spooky, I tell you.

What're you doing here in Lot 4, Block 48, I asked. I don't recall sending out invitations.

It was my understanding, he said, that the white flag out front was a certain message in my direction.

That's when I knew you, Jolene, had been up to some tricks while I was busy pursuing nostalgia. But I didn't let on to your dad that it wasn't me tied that handkerchief. Meaning what? I asked him.

What?

White flag meaning what, I'm asking you.

He had to think that one over, your dad. What he had to gain and what he had to lose. He had to think that over for a bit but then he came out with it. Cease-fire, he said, is what I understand is being indicated.

That's right, I said. This is a cease-fire truce we seem to have here.

By this time we were sitting on the sofa like old times.

You're looking fine, I said, to indicate I was good as my word and holding my ammunition.

A man has to keep up appearances, he said. Then, the same for you.

A woman can't relax her standards.

He moved closer at that point. You could do worse, he said, than yours truly.

What's your sudden interest in my life, I asked. I thought she was the point, I said, meaning you. I thought our girl was the point.

She was not the point, he said. Okay, she was *a* point, maybe, but not *the* point. She's my blood kin, so I had a duty. But you're my wife. Don't you see? A man has a duty to his blood kin, but his wife, that's a choice.

Since when did you remember you had a wife?

Since the last twenty-one years, that's when.

That didn't make me back away. That's news, I said.

Come on home, Midge, he said. It's time you led a normal life.

What's a normal life, I ask you? I asked him. What's a normal life in this day and time. Selling oil rig equipment when there aren't any oil rigs? That's normal? I want to see the world, at least the U.S.A. part of same. Twenty-one years I haven't so much as left the great state of Texas, looking after our girl, making sure you couldn't come after me across the border with a warrant. I want to see the rest of it; there's adventure out there.

Where's adventure? he asked me. Out where?

For instance, I said, in the state of Connecticut they

have discovered a canoe-shaped channel of gold right smack under the ground. The thing is to spot the trees that sweat gold traces; just go for the 'burb with the right bark in the backyard and you've got yourself a gold mine. That's adventure. That's a new horizon. I always say a move should provide an education.

The gold mine is sounder than the oil well, he conceded.

Those places up there still have an interest in piano teachers, I encouraged him. They still like their girls (boys, too, I said) to learn the scales, to have a certain polish.

Sounds like a normal life to me, he said.

You got a car that works? I asked him.

Salesman has to.

I've got a set of maps.

That could come in handy.

We sealed it with a kiss.

Where's she gone? he asked me. Our girl, meaning you.

Time will tell, I said.

I did my best.

Your best was real good. You were a stabilizing influence.

You showed her the sights.

Our job's done, I guess you could say.

Looks that way. Between us, he said, I was running out of steam.

Entre nous, I told him, the same here.

And then the rest of it was just mushy stuff and you don't need to hear about that. But imagine this, your mom and dad going off on a second honeymoon in a bright red Chevy Nova that's waxed till it could pass for a Corolla. Going off generic as any old married couple taking the grand tour.

More than likely when we've seen it all we'll be back—ready to settle down in Chillicothe.

Love,
M——

44

"I'M HOME."

"What kept you?"

"This and that."

Henry is in his drawstring pants; I've slipped into my lizard shoes.

"Want some cocoa?" he asks.

"Not now. Now I want to do it sitting up and then I want to do it leaning over the table, and this time *I* get to knock the vase over and the flowers off."

"I've created a monster," he says, sounding glad to see me.

"You created *who?*"

Henry checks me out up close to see where I am. Still touchy, he decides. "Her," he says, gesturing to a stack of clippings about our show.

"That's right, *Jolene*. You created her. Not me."

"You got a lot of phone messages," he says.

"Celebrities don't have to return calls."

"You saw we made the cover?" He holds up the *Newsweek*.

I think about that *we*, who all it could mean, and decide it's okay. "Me and everybody else in town," I tell him.

"I called your aunt's house for you."

"I went to see L.W."

"The actor. The necrophiliac."

"Actually, I went to see his play."

"Was it good?"

"No."

That makes him want to do it, too.

We do it sitting up and we do it with the flowers and vase, and we do it under the covers like a married couple, complete with cocoa in the HIS and HERS cups. Then, because those were all his ideas before, we do it another way that I invent, in the studio, using the black cape that I wore to the show. And all the time we're doing it when I say, and moving on to something else when I'm ready, and we don't stop until I'm out of breath and out of interest and ready to be wrapped in the sheet.

"I'm thinking of a new series," Henry says, because of course he's been painting in his head the whole time we were making love. "With the articulated skeletons. The graveyard band."

He gets out a catalogue from the Mexican Folk Art exhibit to show me, and for a minute it makes me really mad, that all the time I was hiding up there behind the papier-mâché bones, crying and going to pieces about being downstairs on eight walls for the whole world to see, he was taking time to pick up a catalogue just in case. But then I decide that if there's going to be another show, this time I want some of the ideas to be mine.

"I liked the crocodile head and the tiger's mask," I tell him.

He is busy sketching something out on a piece of paper, so I ask him, Did you hear me, and he says yes. "I liked you in the tiger's mask," he says.

"I want to play with the hands."

He looks up. "The Fine Arts show is moving to Washington, that's why I was trying to get hold of you."

"Will we go to the opening?"

"In the fall."

"I want to be the Indian this time."

"In the fall," he says. "I'm going to be paired with someone." He doesn't look pleased. He flips open the magazine and shows me the picture of the kid curled up on the floor by a houseplant, which I've already seen in Humana Hospital. "A Brit. They're still beating the theme about live models. They think in generalities."

"Do you mind? Him being there, too?"

"If it had to be someone, he's fine. He's good; he's different."

"I want to go as the Indian next time," I say again because he didn't answer me.

"Do you?" He looks as if he might smile but he doesn't. He messes with what he was drawing again and then he holds it up for me to see. It's a tiger's face he's done with colored chalk.

"I want to play with the hands," I tell him.

"Now?"

"Now."

He gets them all out on the bed for me. I put them back in the drawer and then get them all out again for myself.

There is the very first young one with the tiny white half-moons, the porcelain one that looks like an old china doll's hand. Then there are two that must have been from when she was in grade school. One has a cut on the back, a real cut, like something scratched the hand; another has a Band-Aid that covers a real tear. Both of these are worn down on the sides of the palms from years of leaning them on desks. Then there are the bigger ones with bigger knuckles and the skinlike gloves that come way up the wrist, the ones that work like real hands, that have a metal cord inside you pull to open the thumb and finger so you can pick things up. The lady ones with small but visible veins and long red fingernails.

I get a little bowl of cold water and the tiny brush that's used for cleaning them. Then, when I have wiped them dry, I line them up in order and, one by one, try them on and grow her up.

"I want them to be mine," I tell Henry.

That makes him have to talk about something else—about how he wants me to have fifty percent of the Jolene pictures, and how I'll get a lot more than that from the offers that are pouring in. That he's sorry about springing the pictures on me; that he's sorry I went crazy. I know that mostly he means that he's sorry I've asked for something he doesn't want to part with.

"I want the hands," I say. "I want them not just to play with but to have. I want them to be mine."

"You can get them out whenever you want."

"*Have*, Henry."

I can see he's having a lot of trouble with this idea. Thinking that if he loses me he'll lose them and then maybe, this is the way his mind works, he'll lose his old daddy who couldn't read and write and his uncle and the camera and the mistress, and there will be a great hole in things that all the losses will leak out. I can see he's thinking that maybe if he gives me the hands he'll have nothing left of himself and will be the bony boy again named Henry Kraft whose mother is shedding the ways of a ranch hand's wife in Denver, Colorado.

But I don't let myself be talked out of wanting them by the look on his face. "Own them," I say.

"What if this doesn't work out?"

"What doesn't work out? Us? We already did. We already did work out, Henry. Are you saying what if we don't end up together in a condo on the coast of Florida sending cards to all our folks?" And I have to laugh at that, being reminded of Mom and her stream of postcards from every little town in Texas.

"Okay," Henry says.

He cuts out the tiger's face and then the eye holes and ties some yarn at the sides and puts it on me, a paper mask.

"To get the idea," he says. He is already moving toward the easel, not even thinking that it's the middle of the night and we've just settled something important. He's not thinking about any of that now because he's on automatic.

I don't mind. I shake myself out to loosen up. I like this two-story glass-walled room when it's pitch-black outside and the bamboo hedge keeps it private and we can't hear a sound anywhere in the house or in the city. It feels good to let time spread out and things stand still.

I try to remember what it was like up there in the museum when I was standing behind the skeleton with my arms and legs all at angles, when I was crying behind the mask with the real boar bristles and there were other faces around me made from human hair and leather, rags and glass—snouts and teeth and ears and beaks. When, past me down the aisle, there were riders on straw donkeys, hats on clay monkeys, wedding veils on sugar skulls. I try to remember what it felt like to hide there with Henry beating that drum.

The last time, all the pictures were in Henry's head; I didn't see them. I wasn't here. I wasn't anywhere here; I left my body for him to use the way the museum person had the hides and limbs and costumes to arrange in rows and cases, the way the real animals and true dancers were somewhere else.

This time I am going to be here.

Still wearing the tiger's face, I get two of the uncle's woman's hands and hold them out in front of me. I scratch the air with them until I can tell that Henry knows that they are paws with claws, then I pound them up and down in the air until I have a rhythm going, until I'm sure he understands the paws are beating the skins. Then I drop the sheet to the floor so I have nothing on but the mask, the hands, and the reptile shoes making iguana feet, and I can see the picture we're doing as clear as day, as clear as if it was already hanging big as life in Washington, D.C.

It feels good just to stand here again not paying any attention to anybody with nobody paying any attention to me.

I'm ready to pose.

A NOTE ABOUT THE AUTHOR

Shelby Hearon was born in Marion, Kentucky, in 1931. She grew up in Kentucky but later moved to Texas, where she was graduated from the University of Texas at Austin in 1953. Over the years she has taught at a number of universities, including American Studies at the University of Texas at Austin, and creative writing at the University of Houston, Bennington College, and the University of California at Irvine. She was the recipient of an Ingram Merrill grant in 1987, a National Endowment for the Arts Creative Writing Fellowship in 1983, the John Simon Guggenheim Memorial Fellowship for Fiction in 1982, and has five times won the NEA/PEN Syndication Short Story Prize and twice won the Texas Institute of Letters best novel award. This is Miss Hearon's eleventh novel. She and her husband, Bill Lucas, live in Westchester County, New York. She has a grown daughter and son.

A NOTE ON THE TYPE

The text of this book was set in a digitized version of Electra, a typeface designed by W. A. Dwiggins for the Mergenthaler Linotype Company and first made available in 1935. Electra cannot be classified as either "modern" or "old style." It is not based on any historical model, and hence does not echo any particular period or style of type design. It avoids the extreme contrast between "thick" and "thin" elements that marks most modern faces, and is without eccentricities which catch the eye and interfere with reading. In general, Electra is a simple, readable typeface which attempts to give a feeling of fluidity, power, and speed.

Composed by Creative Graphics, Inc.,
Allentown, Pennsylvania
Printed and bound by Fairfield Graphics,
Fairfield, Pennsylvania
Typography and binding design by
Iris Weinstein